These Vicious Thorns

Tales of the Lovely Grim

Candace Robinson

For those who wanted to be given a story

Thorna

The world could be a vicious thing, one surrounded by sharpened thorns. Both visible and invisible. For Thorna, this was more than true. She was in love with a human, and she hadn't known true love until she stumbled upon *him*. Lovers of her past had held pieces of her heart, but not her entire being. Thorna had once read a book of dark and monstrous tales called *Dearest Clementine* that she had discovered at an antique store in the mortal world. Inside the tome, a fiend had penned stories to his lover while searching for and trying to save her. It was a book that had stuck with Thorna. And this was her inspiration of how she would attempt to woo the human she loved. For a week, Thorna would bring Asher one story a night before revealing her true self. Then he could decide if he would accept her as she was, including all the beasties of her fae world.

"Just steal him from his world and bring him here," Pyrka said, his jet-black hair brushing his hunched shoulders. He reminded her a little of the Hunchback of Notre Dame in the mortal world, only, Pyrka's flesh resembled tree bark.

Thorna cocked her head and reclined in her throne—made of twisted tree branches—and studied her favorite beastie. Pyrka's eyes glowed a deep gold and thorns ran across his forehead, shoulders, and arms. All the beasties in her throne room were no taller than her waist, yet they could still easily protect and guard her. But Pyrka was her favorite—he was her best friend.

"This is one mortal I would like to give a choice to. Not steal him." She sighed, staring at the room around her. The tangled thorn branches, the colorful butterflies, the high ceiling entwined with violet and cerulean leaves. Behind her, the wall of pale purple water shimmered, falling in tranquil waves into the pond below. Its music was a constant reminder of the portal to the mortal world it held. Taking Asher would be a simple task. But no, she wouldn't resort to that.

Pyrka bowed. "If you need me to retrieve him in the future, I will, my queen."

Thorna patted his head and smiled. "Take leave and see your family for the night." With that, she shifted into her Luna moth form, then darted through the water wall and slipped into the mortal world.

As she flew into the cool night, above the tops of trees and across city lights, Thorna eventually stumbled upon a quaint street filled with two-story brick homes. Asher's old rusty truck sat outside his pristine house, the lights still on in his downstairs window.

Thorna had never been inside Asher's house, only followed him home one day from his work, in her moth form, to see where he lived. It was so she could give him these tales of hers. He loved reading and watching dark fantasy, so she wanted to provide him with something special, endearing.

Wings fluttering, Thorna peered into the glass, through a slit in the blinds, finding Asher alone on a leather couch, his eyes shut. Asher's dark hair was swept back, the lamp highlighting his olive complexion. He was twenty-seven years of age, centuries younger than her, but it didn't matter.

Her heart gave a jerk at the sight of him, just as it had when she first stumbled upon him at the antique shop he owned.

For the past few months, she had come in almost every day. After he had recently asked her on a date, it was time for him to discover who and what she truly was before she told him yes. Thorna wouldn't hide her true nature from any lover.

Shifting into her fae form, her silk dress swishing around her legs, Thorna pushed her emerald hair over her shoulder and retrieved the first story, rolled into a scroll, from the satchel. She set it on the porch mat, along with a twig of thorns atop. Taking a breath, she rang the doorbell, then vanished into the night. For seven nights, she would bring him a new story.

In search of old teacups, Thorna opened the door to the antique shop. She wanted to add more to the collection in her palace. Her collection of things constantly changed, depending on her mood.

"Do you need some help?" a deep voice asked.

She glanced up to find a young mortal sitting behind the desk of the store. He was tall, pretty, but not too pretty, yet not hideous either. His smile was radiant, crooked and imperfect. She liked the way his unruly dark hair flopped into his deep brown eyes, the way his long fingers tapped the desk.

"Perhaps." She shrugged and sauntered toward him.

Lullaby of Flames

*C*ori sat on her bed, strumming a tune on her guitar. It was already dark outside and her parents would be coming home late from her dad's company party. Her brother was out somewhere with his pregnant girlfriend, so it was just Cori, the guitar, an old movie playing in the background, and her black and white checkered vinyl dress. Vintage.

She placed one platformed boot on the carpet. These babies were several inches off the floor and the tops reached right below her knee. She looked awesome, she felt awesome—no one at school thought she was awesome. No teardrops would fall on her guitar, though.

After playing the strings once more, Cori set the instrument down to reach for her phone and look at the time. "It's 9:58 PM on a Saturday night and I'm queen of the world!" she screamed at the top of her lungs, just because she could.

Releasing a sigh and a somewhat amused laugh, Cori bounced on the bed to finish watching *Romy and Michele's High School Reunion* for the gazillionth time. Without her guitar, she still had to keep her hands busy, so she grabbed her crochet hook and yarn from the side table, then started weaving. The piece in her hands looked to be a bear—one eye, no nose, mouth or other eye because she couldn't figure out how to make her way back to that area.

"My favorite part!" Cori waved the crochet hook vigorously at the TV. "Yes, Romy, you invented those Post-Its!" Cori was raised on oldies, but goodies, and that was why she had a hard time connecting with anyone. Most days, she felt out of place, a tortoise in its shell, a hidden pearl in a clam, but she had to pretend to be outgoing.

Her phone dinged and she grabbed it, needing some potential human to interact with at this intense moment in her existence. Instead, it was just the salon's automatic text confirming her hair appointment for the next day. She should've known. Oh well, tomorrow her hair would be a bright flaming orange, chopped in a bob with blunt bangs. *Times will be a changin'.*

With a clap, Cori bounced up and down on the bed. "Social media stats time." She drummed with one hand on her knee and the other flicking to each site of her social media accounts. 15 followers. 27 followers. 2 followers. She sighed. Her band was getting nowhere, and by *band*, she meant her solo act. It wasn't her fault she had a problem talking to people. Even the people who did seem intrigued at first weren't interested in what she wanted to play, so solo act it would be—for now.

Even her brother, Ryan, and his girlfriend—who was about to pop from the growing baby—could still go out and be social at a party on this lame day of the week.

Cori was eighteen, graduating next week, and would be starting summer college courses soon. Maybe her life would pick up then.

"Back to business," Cori sang, as soon as "Time After Time" came on during the movie. She lifted her pearly white guitar and let her fingers fly across the strings. The moment she did, the floor, the cement, the dirt—all of it beneath her feet *shook.*

"Whoa," she whispered, softly stumbling back, her legs striking the bed and making her knees buckle. The mattress saved her. She peered down at the pick in between her fingers. "I did this." Her stare flicked to the window with a starry-eyed gaze. "I'm like, a goddess or something."

Before she could strum the guitar again, the ground shook once more. All of her dollar store Jesus candles vibrated on the shelf. "Possibly not me then." She turned her attention to the potential higher being. "Jesus?"

When no answer came, she quickly tore the guitar from her body and placed it on her bed. She stumbled through her pile of dirty shirts, yanked up the blinds, and pushed up the window. The night sky was dark, except for the whole two stars attempting to light it up. A moon lay hidden somewhere, trying to play hide and seek.

Through the open window, Cori strained her eyes as best she could, but didn't catch a glimpse of anything strange—only the twitching of the tree limbs moving with the wind. The backyard had too many trees that were planted by the previous owners, causing a collision of roots to be cramped together. Shrugging, she rested her fingers on the window, intending to close it, when a small sizzle came from near one of the trees. It almost sounded like meat cooking on the grill.

Tapping her lip, she knew it was time to play detective. Besides, she had her heavy-duty boots on if she needed to kick someone between the legs—male or female. Cori fumbled for her phone and switched on the flashlight. She didn't want to waste time by going into the kitchen to grab some matches to light one of her Jesus or Mary candles. It wasn't the 1800s. Although, she kind of wished it was.

As she climbed out her window, the sizzling sound remained constant. She imagined an intruder with his or her hands up, wiggling their fingers, as if saying *come to me*. Well, she was going to check out whatever it was. A person couldn't make the ground shake like that anyway … at least, not a normal-sized person.

The wind brushed against her body with a cool touch. Cori's forehead wrinkled and her eyebrows shot down as she stared at where the noise was coming from. The flashlight on her phone hit a spot on the ground just right, in front of the old Oak tree with her retired wooden swing swaying side to side. *Squeak. Squeak.*

Biting her lip, she looked from side to side, and saw nothing. But then the sizzling escalated, and she took a shaky step back. She clenched her phone so hard that she feared it would break.

The ground vibrated and lifted a fraction, making a glowing orange light peep through an almost rectangular slot where grass met dirt. Was someone cooking below ground? Aliens? *Oh, please let it be aliens and take me out of this shitty era to, like, 1975.*

Cori inched closer and the ground stopped shaking, the glowing orange vanishing. Did she imagine it? She knelt to the moistened grass and brushed her hand across the surface until it collided with the open space where the brightness had shone through.

With one quick lift, Cori threw the dirt lid up and let the light on her phone fire below. Maybe there was a secret basement in her backyard that she and her family hadn't known existed. Dead bodies. A previous owner had thrown dead bodies down here. That *had* to be it!

Down the hole, she couldn't see anything except for

dirt walls. She needed to go inside the house and find a stronger flashlight. First and more importantly, she needed to check something on her phone. Right when she was about to Google paranormal activity, murderers, and locate a priest, the ground shifted, launching her forward. She lost her balance, falling, down, down, down, flapping her arms like a dying bird.

When people fall to their supposed deaths, they should shout, right? Well, I can't seem to get a word out. Cori let the bats—because that was what they had to be, couldn't be butterflies in this death trap—float around her stomach as she dropped into darkness. But the obscurity didn't last for long, instead switching to an orange flickering.

The air around her shifted, causing Cori's descent to slow. She found it difficult to move, as though she was sluggishly dancing. *If dancing is thumping onto the ground....* But she didn't smack it. Her body jostled and when her feet touched the pebbled dirt, she fell back, her skull striking the ground. Head spinning, she stared up, up, up. The entrance banged shut, and the ominous sound echoed down, down, down to Cori. Her eyes watched in horrified fascination when the top of the hole lowered until it was just a dirt ceiling several feet above her head.

The realization—the answer—was that she had died. And she didn't even get to live to see her social media account grow to great heights, or have the people at her school discover that she was a cool kind of strange, not just strange. *Oh. Well.* Yet her heart deflated because she wouldn't get to see her brother's girlfriend pop out Cori's baby niece. She wouldn't get to meet and teach the baby all the facts that floated inside her head on a daily basis.

What now?

"I see an angel fell, but I'm sorry to say you're not in Heaven, darlin'," a male voice said.

Cori jerked forward, prepared to strike the guy in between the legs and maybe destroy his penis with the kick if she had to.

"Whoa, now, darlin'." He chuckled and stumbled back.

"Don't you *darlin'* me, you, you—" She had her leg halfway pulled back to hit him when she froze. What the hell was he wearing?

The guy was around her age—holding his hands up in surrender—and dressed in a decades-old army green military uniform, tan boots rising up to his mid-calves, and a rifle of sorts strapped to his back. His dark hair was brushed over to the side, and he stretched out a hand to Cori's. She didn't grab it. Narrowing her eyes at his hazel ones, she rose to her full height and gave him the glare of death. She was smaller than him, but he seemed to get the hint.

Shrugging, he waved her over. "If you're smart, then I suggest you follow me."

"Hmm… I guess I'm not smart then, because I'm not going anywhere with you." She pointed to the ceiling above. "I'm going back out the way I came."

A rumbling sounded from behind her—she was prepared to scale the damn wall, then crawl on the ceiling to the center to get the fuck out of wherever she was. But the tunnel was *gone* and wasn't reforming. In the distance, the sound grew stronger, louder, a cloud of dust presenting itself. In that dust, two dogs appeared. Dogs with *flames*. Dogs with two heads. Dogs with devil-horned beasts riding them. Roars escaped all four dog heads—showcasing rows of sharp teeth—and making her ears throb. The beasts riding the dogs had the body of a man with a muscular size that shouldn't exist on anyone, and a face that would put any comic book villain to shame. The tips of their horns could pluck out her eyes in a heartbeat.

"Holy shit!" Cori shouted, still clenching her phone, even after the fall.

Her body was glowing a soft lilac color. Hurriedly, Cori turned back around to tell the strange guy that she would go with him to the ends of the earth if he so requested, but his ass was gone. No, not gone, but farther in the distance and leaping onto a silver canoe. On each side, tall tips curved their way up into a spiral on top. The canoe started moving and the army-dressed guy stuck out his hand when she ran over, also glowing purple. She clasped his calloused fingers and he hauled her in.

Cori landed with a thump, making the canoe sway unsteadily. "You left me behind!"

"I told you to come on!" He matched her level of exaggeration as he took a seat in front of her.

"But you didn't say there were monstrous dogs with beastly devils who have flames all over their bodies!"

He made an annoying click with his tongue and cocked his head. "There wasn't time for all that."

"Why are we purple?" As soon as she said that, the glow went away.

"They are luring your soul out to be reaped for their favorite demon."

Demon... Cori wouldn't look back. She would *never* look back. And yet...

She totally looked back and studied the beasts standing at the edge of the water, trying not to douse out their flames—or so she guessed. Yet the roaring from all of them continued, converging into a sound she'd never heard before. She covered her ears as—what was his name?—started rowing.

Tearing her stare away from the beasties, she turned to face said guy, and glanced down at his hands. He wasn't rowing. Who the fuck was rowing? *No one, that's who.* She stood up and the boat shook, so she sat back down and watched frantically as the oars moved by themselves. This was either the worst, or best, dream ever. She couldn't decide as her eyes made pyramid shapes from army guy, to oars, to water, to beasts, and back again.

"What's going on?" Cori fanned herself with the neck of her dress as her temperature rose and a sheen of sweat formed on her face. "Is it hot in here, or is it just me?"

"Well, darlin'," the guy started, "since you asked so nicely… It just so happens to be your lucky day that I found you on my way to the entrance."

Cori looked down at her phone, which showed no reception. She tried to get on Google or any site, but nothing worked. It should've been expected since she was so far below ground, or wherever she was. Despite the messed-up things that were going on, she tried to focus on this guy to get some answers.

"Are we dead?" She'd hit her head on the fall, but she never blacked out or anything of that nature.

"No, but you might end up so." His tone sounded almost sorry about the whole scenario.

"What does that even mean? Where are we? Who are you?"

He pointed to the ceiling of … her head slowly tilted upward … *flames.*

Then she thought about where she'd fallen, which appeared to be more of an island since it was surrounded by water. Hell. She was in Hell. "You said I wasn't in Heaven because... We're in Hell!"

"You guessed it." The guy ran a hand through his hair and blew out a hard breath.

She scooted as far back as she could. "And let me guess, you're Satan."

He smirked. "If that were true, then I'd have opened up that entrance and we'd both be out of here."

"Was one of those creatures back there him?"

Shaking his head, he waved a hand around the room. "Don't worry, the Devil is here somewhere."

"Then, again, who are you? Explain to me what's going on." Cori studied the canoe as the oars moved by themselves, wishing it was an odd special effect so she could twitch her lips and feel amused.

"Darlin', are you sure you want to know?" He said it in a way that implied it was a story he'd told many times before. The undertone of his voice also implied people couldn't handle it, as if *she* couldn't handle it.

"*Darlin'*"—she clenched her teeth—"tell me before I kick your ass."

He rolled his eyes, but then they widened when they landed on her boots. "Those do look like weapons. Anyway, my name is Rigel Samuel Lampkin. I was fighting in World War 1 during 1917 and stumbled across the gateway to Hell. While war is hell, this is much, much worse."

Did he say World War 1? Lips parted and leaning closer, she stared at his boyish face, getting a good look for the first time. No wrinkles, no graying hair, no sagging skin. In actuality, he was fit as a damn fiddle.

Handsome even—which would be the proper word to use if he really was from the early 1900s. "Sorry, I don't believe that. Unless … you're a ghost? You'd be decrepit and bones by now."

"I was sixteen when I fell down and am eighteen now. I've only been down here a couple of years," he said, like it was no big deal what they were discussing.

"Try over a hundred years!" she whisper-shouted. This guy, Rigel, was in denial.

He didn't seem surprised. "Since I've been down here, I've learned that time works differently. People fall into this pit quite often—before me, after me."

Cori let that sink in and didn't say anything. She stared around the murky brown water and the rest of the place. Besides the flaming fire on the ceiling, it looked more like a normal forest. She would've expected Hell to be bare bones and rotting trees, but it all appeared healthy.

"I know what you're thinking, but his lair is where things are supposedly worse." Rigel paused. "And you still haven't told me *your* name?"

"Oh, sorry. It's Cori." All she could focus on was what the Devil's lair would have in it. A blackened mansion with flames and weapons? Possibly goat heads or other animal heads strung on strings to decorate the place?

She didn't have time to think much more on the subject because the canoe struck what looked to be plain old dirt. "Where are we—"

"Rigel, we didn't think you were going to make it!" a girl shouted, wearing a striped dress that looked straight from the 50s. Her hair was pulled into an out-of-style curled updo.

Cori didn't have time to focus on how much she wanted that dress before Rigel spoke, "What's going on now?"

"So … the demons' daddy is already out and about." The girl's mahogany eyes landed on Cori. "Now I know why. He'll be here to play soon."

"Satan?" Cori asked, prepared for the ceiling of flames to lower down around her. Why hadn't she stayed inside her room? Why did she have to go investigate?

"He doesn't go by Satan down here, too good for that." Rigel shook his head. "Just the Devil, and he's apparently hungry already."

"Charming," Cori said with sarcasm, "and stupid." Anyone who would go by "the" in front of their name thought too highly of themselves.

"Cori"—he motioned between the two girls—"meet Barbara."

At that specific moment, zombie movies came to mind. "They're coming to get you, Bar-ba-ra."

"What?"

"Never mind." Clearly, Barbara didn't understand the movie reference, and that was okay.

"We need to hurry!" Barbara said, her eyes wild and searching. Clasping Cori's wrist, Barbara dragged her across the dirt. Cori kind of wanted to kick this girl between the legs, too, for how hard she was yanking her arm.

Around them, the trees swayed violently as if a storm was brewing. The flames above Cori crackled like thunder.

An *eek, eek, eek* boomed just ahead. A storm of birds—no, bats lit in flames—crashed through the trees, flapping their wings with a tremendous smacking. The wing of one struck Cori across the side of her neck, and a hot flame bit into her skin. Quickly, she placed her hand over the throbbing spot. As the bats trickled away, a man in red appeared in front of them.

"I told you not to go out, Rigel!" Barbara shouted. And somehow from those words, Cori knew this predicament was all because of her slowing Rigel down.

"I've got one bullet left, and it's the best I got." Rigel tugged the gun from his back, and aimed it at the man.

All Cori had was the phone—that didn't work—still gripped fiercely in her hand.

"New meat," the man or should she say, costume wearer, said. It was so obvious that this was "the Devil." The lord of the demons, with his thin black mustache, looked as if he was ready for a costume party, raven-colored pitchfork in clawed hand. A red bodysuit clung to the Devil's lanky form from toe to horned head. At his tailbone, a tail flicked side to side, putting the arrowhead tip on display.

Cori's camera still worked, and she was two seconds from bringing the phone up to take a picture, when he thrust his pitchfork against the ground, causing it to rumble. "Get them, minions!" he bellowed.

Minions? Cute, yellow creatures came to mind, but no, they resembled half-sized werewolves crawling out from the ground. Cori and her companions started to glow the soft lavender, like before. She didn't think. She geared up with her phone like she used to when her mom made her play softball. Then she threw the device rough and hard, hitting bullseye via the Devil's nose. Too bad she hated softball, though.

The action bought them enough time for Rigel to scoop Cori over his shoulder, and carry her to wherever the hell he and Barbara were fleeing to.

"Release me!" Cori yelled.

"You don't know where we're going, and you'll only slow us down," he rasped.

Their bodies continued to glow with a purple aura, and she tried to perform an inner struggle, begging her soul to stay put if a demon latched on.

A werewolf demon with sharp triangular ears and flames for fur caught up with Rigel. Cori couldn't see where Barbara was. With a hard pull, Cori made Rigel twist to the side, causing them both to fall. She hauled back her leg and shoved her boot against the beast's face. But another one appeared and clamped its paws on her ankle. Inside her, something burned hot while being torn away—her soul. Just in time, with her other boot, she clomped the beast's head and the sucker unlatched, freeing her.

Two strong hands hauled her up—Rigel. "Don't do that again," he said as he pulled Cori in a direction between two lush trees. Barbara was ahead, trying to outrun them. Behind Cori, the howls of the wolves sounded as though they were drawing closer—she didn't chance a glance back.

Her gaze focused on two large rocks in the shape of blackened horns and what looked to be a doorway. She was about to turn around when Rigel said, "Sanctuary."

Cori prepared herself as she collided through the open entrance for the unknown. But what she found was a spacious empty area with two other girls standing near the back.

Out of breath, Barbara turned around and placed her hands on Rigel's cheeks, checking him for wounds. *Boyfriend?* Cori guessed. But then Barbara patted his head as if he was her child. *Maybe a messed-up relationship?*

Barbara turned to Cori and tilted her head to the side to inspect the wound on Cori's neck. "You're lucky that's all you got."

The roars of the demons outside diminished, as if they were giving up. *Why wouldn't they just storm through the open space?*

"What took you guys so long?" a girl with permed hair strolled forward, interrupting Cori's thoughts.

"Yeah?" The other girl with bell-bottomed jeans asked, but didn't come any closer.

"We rescued," Barbara began, "or rather, Rigel found a newbie."

The girl with the permed hair opened her mouth in awe. "It's been a while. They've all been getting reaped so quickly lately."

"I don't feel very lucky," Cori said, staring at each of the strangers' faces, feeling more and more out of place by the second. More so than at school.

"What year did you come from?" Permed Hair asked, grabbing a lock of Cori's long ponytail—the one that was supposed to get chopped off tomorrow morning. From the looks of things, that wouldn't be happening now.

"2020," Cori answered, remembering what Rigel said about him being from World War 1.

"Holy shit!" Permed Hair grinned. "That has to be the year of the beast. People still dress like this? It looks as if you're from the same decade as me."

Cori peered down at her vinyl checkered dress that was probably actually from the 90s. It had been in the back of her mother's closet, along with other saved clothing that was decades old. Cori had taken most of them out to wear. "It's actually my mom's. What year are you guys from?"

Barbara answered, "1954."

"1975, and you can call me Deb," Bell Bottoms said.

Permed Hair replied last. "1997, and my name's Tracy."

A smile crossed Cori's face, the first one since she'd fallen down the hole of beasts. "Wow, I said I wanted to get transported back to 1975."

"Figure a way out of here," Deb said, "and you can come."

At that moment, she had a sinking feeling. If they did crawl out, everyone would be in the year 2020. Time had already passed. "I'm Cori."

Rigel walked away and looked out of the cave but kept both feet planted inside.

"How are we in a sanctuary if this is the 'Devil's playground?'" Cori asked, stepping away from the group of girls. She'd never felt so overcrowded in her life.

Slowly turning around, Rigel leaned his back on the wall of the cave. "A man named Robert, God rest his soul"—Rigel did something that was supposed to be the sign of the cross but looked more like he was playing tic tac toe with the air—"was very biblical and he blessed this place when he first fell down here."

"Where is he now?" There was no one else in the large space.

"He didn't make it," Tracy answered.

"I'm sorry." Cori sighed. Then her stomach gurgled when her gaze met a large stack of apples in a corner that looked like a miniature hill. "Is that what you guys have to eat here?"

Rigel moved to the corner and tossed her an apple,

biting into one himself.

She easily caught the fruit and rolled it over and over. "Very Adam and Eve."

"Very Adam and Lilith," Tracy answered.

"What?" Cori asked, watching as Barbara and Deb went to have a seat and eat their apples.

"Lilith was the snake in the story," Rigel said, "not Satan. She was pissed because Adam had taken a new wife after their happily ever after was not so happy. Lilith was the first wife."

Cori ran her gaze along the vaulted ceiling and the stone walls. "So she should join the First Wives Club then?"

"What?" Rigel asked, eyebrows lowered in confusion.

She rolled her eyes. "Never mind."

Running a hand through his hair, Rigel sank to the floor and reclined against the wall. Cori sat down beside him, while Tracy grabbed an apple and lowered herself next to Barbara.

Barbara leaned forward and watched Cori still fiddling with the apple. "It's not poisoned. And even if it was, there's nothing else to eat. But we haven't died yet, if that helps."

Nonchalantly, Cori brought the red fruit to her face. Peer pressure could be a bitch, but she *was* hungry. She bit in and found it to be just fine, if a bit dry.

After finishing their apples, the other three girls laid down and closed their eyes. Only she and Rigel were left sitting, Cori still trying to finish her not-very tasty apple. She figured she might as well ask more questions. "So, how do you know about Lilith?"

Rigel set down his apple core and ran a hand across

his jaw, then pointed to her almost-eaten fruit. "She's at the apple tree where we gather those."

Mid-swallow, Cori couldn't control herself from choking on the piece, and it continued to stay lodged in her throat. Rigel hauled her forward and did some shit to her back with a hard slap, and the chunk flew out.

He lifted her chin. "Next time, darlin', chew slower."

She was over that apple after another near-death experience, and set the rest to the side. "What do you mean at the tree?"

"I told you Lilith was the snake, and she's permanently in that form now. Or so she says, anyway."

Cori had always believed that there was some higher being out there. She'd just never been sure what kind. Her collection of religious candles at home were mostly for decoration purposes, and because they had looked cool. However, she did know the basics.

"All I know about Lilith is that she's a demon and apparently a baby snatcher." She paused for a moment, because one of her favorite movies came to mind. "Sounds like Jareth from *Labyrinth*."

"I love that movie!" Tracy shouted.

"Who?" Rigel asked.

Every time he didn't know an answer, she wanted to pat his shoulder in sympathy. "You wouldn't get it." Cori shot Tracy two thumbs up. "I think she's my favorite person down here."

"Hey, but I saved your life!" Rigel chuckled.

"Yet, originally, you also would've left me behind."

"If you have questions," he began, changing the subject, "I can take you to Lilith on our next fruit raid. But be warned, she's a bit on the wordy side."

"I think I'll pass on talking to the demon snake." The

four had been here quite a bit and Lilith had obviously not helped them.

Tiredness hit Cori right then as she covered her mouth to yawn. She would've already been long past sleepville if she'd been at her house. Her parents would be home, her brother and girlfriend would be there, too. But no one would likely notice Cori was gone until morning, unless the baby decided to come that night. She hoped not.

"There are no blankets or anything, but it doesn't get that cold down here." Rigel grinned. "Pun intended."

The light humor helped her to relax as she rested on her back and stared up at the ceiling. He was right—she felt warm and toasty, almost a bit cozy on the dirt floor.

As she lay there, despite the tiredness, Cori couldn't sleep. There weren't any more beastly growls on the outside, but that didn't mean the danger was gone. Among the girls on the other side of the room, Barbara snored loudly, while Tracy and Deb seemed to be deep in sleep, too.

"Can you not sleep?" Rigel asked.

She turned her head to face him and he was already looking in her direction. "No. You?"

"I try not to sleep, but sometimes it overtakes me anyway. When I do, I dream about war. When I'm awake, I think about a different kind of war."

Rigel was the same age as her in terms of when he fell down the hole, yet he'd seen much more hardships than she ever had. What were her worries? Social media followers and finding band members? He'd been in *war*. "If it helps, if we ever get out and you end up in my time, the world is a mess but right now it's mainly wars with people's words on the Internet. And if you don't know what that is, it's basically people who aren't face to face who write words to each other."

"I'm not expecting to go back to my time. And even if I did, I wouldn't have much to go back to anyway. My two sisters died from illnesses, and my pa and ma didn't get along too well with me."

That was another thing Cori hadn't faced. She got along with both her parents and her brother was still alive. She thought about her hobbies and maybe he had one, too. "Was there anything you found enjoyment in?"

"Basketball, piano—"

"Shut up!" She lifted her head and may have leaned a little too close to his face over her excitement. "We can be band members. I mean, I play the guitar, and maybe we can jam sometime together."

He smiled, amusement flashing in his eyes. "Jamming sounds good, darlin'."

Cori's cheeks may have pinkened a little, and she blew out a breath, pointing her head in the direction of the girls. "So which one is your real darlin' over there?"

"Um, all of you?"

"Is this like a harem thing?" She moved back a couple inches. "Because that's cool, but I'm not going to be part of some weird sexual circle."

He let out a deep chuckle, then cleared his throat. "No, no, nothing like that."

"Ah, just a gentleman then."

"Just a gentleman," he echoed with a smile.

Cori rolled to her back and changed the subject. "A fact: we don't have flying cars yet, but we do have phones still, like the one I threw at the Devil's head. It has a camera, calculator, and all types of things that you can use on it. It's like the devil and angel all rolled into one.

People use it like heroin and don't focus on real life at times. It's sad, really."

"I never did like the telephone."

Cori was going to say something, but she noticed Rigel had drifted off. These people had been down here for a very long time. Maybe not as long as time had passed back upstairs, but long nonetheless, and no one had found a way out. Outside, the howls and roars of creatures started up again, and it sounded as if there was a flickering of fire right near the entrance. She leaned forward and crawled to the opening, pursing her lips. The world was most definitely covered in bright orange flames, consuming *everything*.

Her eyes blinked and blinked and *blinked*. Cori wanted to have some sort of emotion, but right now she was in some kind of weird robot mode where she couldn't feel terrified or upset—or anything really, besides surprised. Maybe because it all seemed crazy. Maybe because she wasn't dead yet. Maybe because the Devil looked like a damn cartoon character. How did that loser ever get in charge of anything? A new name came to mind. Lilith…

What she needed was an angel, not another murderous demon.

But…

She perched on her knees and glanced at Rigel.

"Rigel," she whispered. He didn't move. She stood and walked toward him before hunching down to lightly shake his shoulders. In one swift swoop, he was on top of her, his forearm at her throat. When his eyes met hers, he quickly released her like she'd stung him.

"I'm so sorry." He backed up farther away from her.

"No, it's…" It wasn't fine, but she understood. She

covered her right ear to avoid the sounds from outside as he spoke.

"I should have warned you not to touch me if I fell asleep." Rigel ran both hands down his face and lightly tapped his cheeks. "It's… I don't know what it is…"

She knew what it was instantly. Her father had suffered from it after serving in the military. "PTSD. I get it. I'll explain that to you, too. You'll also learn that we have so many more answers these days on things for all sorts of mental illnesses. We can get you help for it."

He nodded, but still looked ashamed when he shouldn't.

"I think I changed my mind. When the world out of this cave stops burning, I want to talk to Lilith."

"We'll have to wait for seven days…"

"Seven days?" she asked, incredulous. Why would they have to be in here for seven days?

"Seven days on, seven days off… That's why we stock up on the apples."

Cori bit her lip, thinking. "It's like how it supposedly took God seven days to create the Earth, like the Devil's wiping this place out and restarting it again?"

"That's been my thought all along."

Cori froze as something else stirred within her. If she was trapped in this cave for seven days and then somehow managed to crawl out of this hell hole of a place, then how much time would've passed at her home? Years? Would her new niece arriving already be older than her? Would her brother be married to his girlfriend? He used to switch girls out like he changed his socks, until he'd knocked this one up. Would her parents be dead?

"This is why I miss Robert," Rigel said. "He was the

smartest of us, but still couldn't manage to find a way out."

"What happened to him?"

"He saved Tracy."

"Oh." What a pathetic word, but what else could she say? She didn't know Robert, but he sounded ultimately brave, or stupid. It could go either way.

"Once the Devil has your soul, there's no getting it back. No matter how good you are." He shifted to lay back down. "Lilith told us that, too."

There was her name again. Demons could lie, right? They weren't like the fae she'd read about in books who couldn't lie, but could twist words. *Who knows if anything Lilith said is even true?*

Closing her eyes, Cori wondered about herself. Was she good? She wasn't bad, but was she truly good? She'd stolen a belt one time at the store because she wanted to see what it was like, but then she buried it in her backyard like a dead body because she was scared the police would come for it. Maybe that sin had triggered the gate to open in the first place? She could totally see that as being the reason why.

"Whatever sins you have on your hands," Rigel continued, "I'm sure mine are a thousand times worse. I've killed men."

"For the right cause," she said, flicking open her eyes.

"But does that make it less of a sin?"

A sin was a sin, no matter how big or small. "No, I guess not. But still…"

"Look, darlin', get a little more rest because if you want to meet Lilith… Then, for the next seven days I'm going to tell you all the stories she shared with us."

The next seven days were rough. Cori felt as if the heat was going to scorch the place, but it didn't, even though each day grew hotter and hotter. Sweat drenched her body from head to toe. Of the three girls, Cori talked to Tracy the most because they liked the same movies and music. Barbara was more on the motherly side, while Deb liked to keep to herself. Cori would watch Rigel the most, though. Throughout the day, he'd polish his gun over and over with a cloth, even though it was cleaned to the max. It seemed to keep him from thinking too much about things.

Rigel then told her about Lilith and all the information she'd given to everyone. There wasn't much more than the things Rigel had already told her. But it was true that Lilith had once had a fetish for taking babies and having sex with any man she so desired.

The days passed slowly, and Cori worried about her family at home, but mostly about how much time she was missing out on. At night, she continued to sleep next to Rigel, but Tracy and the other girls slept closer as they built some kind of bond with Cori.

Before she fell asleep on the seventh day, she looked at Rigel. He was still awake, and she wondered why the guys weren't like him at school—more gentlemanly, more kind, more genuine.

In the morning, a voice whispered her name. She opened her eyes to two hazel irises meeting hers. "The burning's over if you still want to head out to the apple tree, darlin'."

Cori jolted up as her anxiety to find Lilith slammed into her with full force. The girls remained asleep except for Deb.

"I need a break, too," Deb said.

The three of them headed out from the sanctuary and Cori just knew when she looked outside that everything was going to be black and charred. She was wrong. Even though she could still smell the after-effects of the smoke, everything was back to being green and full of life. The Devil must love playing the role of God. *Isn't that what got him here in the first place?*

Above her, the flames burned bright orange with a tinge of blue in what she considered to be the sky. "I'd always thought if there was a Hell, it would look dead and dreary."

"Remember the other day what I told you Lilith spoke of," Rigel said. "The outside may look lively, but on the inside, everything *is* dead. Nothing is as it seems."

She did remember that.

"The Devil isn't as strong as God," Deb said. "So it makes sense that he would be able to create only illusions."

"We need to make it fast." Rigel pointed in a direction wrapping around the cave. "One person is plenty, two is a bit much, and three will draw too much attention."

Deb nodded. "We'll hurry."

The rocky path around the cave and down the hill was quicker than Cori expected. She kept an eye out for anything suspicious.

In the distance, there were howls and roars of what

sounded like animals either mating or killing each other—or possibly both.

At the bottom of the hill stood a single tree, as if the others were frightened to be near it. Cori stopped in her tracks, taking in the bright colors and gorgeousness of it. The leaves shone a luscious green, the bark a healthy brown. Wings flapped in the branches.

Deb shook her head and Cori looked closer. The bats that flew off were not normal bats at all. They were on a larger scale, with three heads attached.

As the trio crept to the tree, Deb folded up her shirt and plucked apples from the branches.

Cori scanned the tree thoroughly, searching for some type of snake. Unless it was camouflaged really well, she didn't see a sign of anything, and she sure didn't hear any hissing. "Where is it?"

"You mean, where is she?" a female voice purred—definitely not Deb.

Holding her breath, Cori gazed steadily at the branch in front of her as a snake with sickly green skin and coffee-colored spots slithered forward.

"Good afternoon, Lilith," Rigel said, ever so gentlemanly as if he wasn't talking to a baby thief.

"Does thou want to come play with me tonight underneath the fire, sweetheart?" Lilith asked in a sultry tone while swirling around and around the branch, perking up her head when she came to a stop near the end.

Rigel rubbed at his temples, for the first time appearing truly annoyed. "You already know I won't give in to that temptation."

Lilith's head drew forward in Cori's direction. "What about you?"

Was she talking about sexual advances with a snake? This demon was all kinds of messed up. "No, but I have another question. I wanted to see if you could help us find a way out of here."

"Now, you know I can't do that." Lilith's tail thumped against the branch. "Everyone has asked me this same question. Why would the answer be any different, Cori?"

The blood in Cori's veins switched from hot to cold. "How do you know my name?"

"I'm a demon. I know many things," Lilith whispered silkily, then she looked up and stopped moving. "Hide."

From behind her, Cori heard the sound of scampering feet—too scattered and clunky to be human. Two creatures with long snouts drew forward, hooting like monkeys. Their floppy ears hung below their hip bones. A purple aura glowed against her skin, as did Rigel's and Deb's. Cori and Rigel darted around to the back of the tree, her back pressed to the bark and Rigel right up against her stomach. For a brief moment, she thought about how nice his body felt against hers—aside from his weapon poking her in the shoulder—but then she came back to reality.

Where was Deb?

A rustling stirred and Deb made a noise akin to a mouse's squeak. Rigel and Cori pushed away from the trunk to help her, but it was already too late. The creatures scurried away with the purple light, while Deb's body collapsed on the ground, right below Lilith. The snake dropped from the tree, landing on top of the still form.

As soon as Lilith connected with the skin, Deb's eyes flicked open. Rigel's gun was already pointed at her head. "I have one bullet. One I was saving, but I can use it at this moment.”

“Oh, put that toy of yours away,” Deb said. “That wouldn’t hold me off for long.”

“Deb?” Cori asked and watched with a quickening heart as the snake previously inhabited by Lilith fell to the ground—dead.

“Lilith, you mean. I’m sorry to say, Deb won’t be returning. And it just so happens I’ve been needing a body. That cursed Devil stole mine away, and I was trapped being that pitiful creature for far too long. Adam. The Devil. I loathe all males.” She looked at Rigel. “Except for you, sweetheart.”

“You tricked us!” Rigel shouted softly, but his facial expression was filled with rage.

“Now, now.” Lilith flicked her hand at Rigel. “That was none of my doing. An empty body happened to fall beneath my tree, so I leapt at the chance. Can’t really blame me for that. Even if I had bitten her, my snake form didn’t contain venom.”

Cori finally found words. “Help us get out of here. I know you have a way.”

Lilith placed her hand against the tree and let out a lazy yawn. “Go and play with the Devil and retrieve his pitchfork. The weapon will open up the gate.”

Rigel balled his hands into fists, his face turning a bright shade of scarlet. “You’ve never told me that before. I’ve been to the tree time and time again, and so have the others.”

“Yet, you never blessed me with a body, or anything to barter.” She glanced at Cori. “Your new friend’s gift to me is exquisite.”

Cori hadn’t known Deb long, but her stomach sank and her chest tightened. This wasn’t going to go over so well with Barbara and Tracy when they brought Lilith in the form of Deb back.

"Now," Lilith pushed away from the tree, running a finger down her chest in between her breasts—"you didn't think that was the end of it, did you? You two will do as I say or I can easily have your souls reaped for the Devil and still manage to get what I want when a new human travels their way down into this pit."

She hated being at the beck and call of this demon woman, but Lilith was providing some answers. "Okay," Cori answered. "You mentioned the pitchfork." The Devil's clawed hand attached to that blackened tool of menace was one image she would never forget. She didn't think she would easily be able to just say, *pardon me, Devil,* and swipe it from his hand.

"Where the Devil stays is surrounded by flame." Lilith lit her own tiny flame on the tip of her index finger and then dismissed it. "I can do things, too."

Holy shit. Lilith could most definitely make her and Rigel burst into flames if she wanted.

"When I come back to the sanctuary," Lilith continued, "you *will not* tell the girls I'm Lilith. No need to risk letting the Devil know I'm back, or the other girls getting a bit feisty."

"Fine," Rigel answered.

"I'm serious," Lilith cooed. "If you think about opening your mouth, I'm known to be able to swipe heads from bodies and juggle them."

Cori's hand automatically went to her throat where her head rested happily attached.

Rigel crossed his arms and moved closer to Cori, as though he was protecting her precious head. "What happened to you calling me sweetheart?"

"That was only when I needed something"—Lilith bared her teeth—"and I got it."

Rigel's vein twitched at his jaw, but he didn't say anything else. He'd known Deb longer than Cori. And Deb may not have talked much, but she hadn't tried to toss out Cori from the cave either.

Cori knew there was more Lilith wanted, but she didn't know what that was yet. But she was sure she would discover it sooner or later.

Lilith walked at a brisk pace, leading them both back to the cave. Quietly, she placed the apples in the corner and gave a wicked smile to Cori and Rigel before whirling around. She turned her lips downward, appearing just as Deb would've.

"We're going to try leaving tomorrow and find a way out of here," Lilith said softly. "All we need is the Devil's pitchfork."

Barbara threw up her hands and looked from Lilith to Cori to Rigel. "What are you talking about?"

"Lilith told us." Cori stared up at the ceiling, trying to sound steady. "You know, the snake in the tree."

"And you believe that crazy bitch?" Tracy shouted, setting an apple down and joining the circle.

Oh, dear lord.

"She's not crazy," Lilith snapped. "And she could kill you all any time she wanted."

"Anyway," Cori said airily to break up the tension, "if you two want to stay here, I understand."

Barbara stepped forward, finger shaking with fury as she pressed it to Cori's chest. "Is that what you want? How do we know you're not Lilith? How do we know you're not the Devil himself? You just came here and magically got words from the snake, when we've been here for so much longer and have tried the same.”

Cori took a deep swallow, controlling herself from shifting her eyes to Lilith. All she could visualize was everyone’s head being juggled by the demon. “I don’t know. Maybe she was in a giving mood.”

“We’re going in the morning,” Rigel said. “Cori isn’t a demon or anything else, and no one’s forcing you to go.”

“And yet, you seem to be under her spell for some reason.” Barbara narrowed her eyes. “You used to think more logically, and now you want to just go and try to break through flames?”

“Lilith blessed us with a way to open the flames and get to the pitchfork,” Cori mumbled.

“You’re lying,” Barbara seethed.

This was true.

“Barbara, just stop,” Tracy interrupted. “You’re the one here being irrational. Maybe we do have a way to get back. I’m going with them.”

Barbara let out a frustrated huff. “Fine, but if I die, Tracy, so help me…”

“It’s settled,” Rigel said, walking away from the circle.

After that, the rest of the day was mainly spent waiting for morning to arrive. At night, Lilith spread her legs out in a very seductive position as she slept. Cori quirked an eyebrow at Rigel while Tracy and Barbara didn’t notice since they were already sleeping beside each other.

Rigel waggled a finger and Cori scooted in until she was pressed against his warmth. He smelled like smoke from a fire. She did, too, and she supposed they all did. But a pleasant outdoorsy scent also radiated from him.

Maybe it was the era he'd come from. She thought again about if they all got out how much the others would have to get used to, but especially him.

"I'm not a demon," she whispered, not really knowing if he'd thought about what Barbara had said.

"I know that." He rolled his eyes. "I'm going to go in for the pitchfork, but you're going to have to be the one to tag along with me. Barbara is too impulsive, and Tracy loses focus easily."

Lilith had mentioned two going in and two staying out with her to break up the possibility of minions locating a group. "You're thinking like someone in the military." Cori nudged his arm.

"We're just a band of misfits, aren't we?" Rigel sighed, his eyes not leaving hers.

She was proud to be considered a misfit, especially a group of ones. The feeling of being left out always consumed her, but being a part of a group of others who felt the same way made her smile. "When we get home, you can stay with me. I'll talk to my parents, and we'll figure out something. I mean, they already let my brother's girlfriend live with us anyway."

Rigel placed his hand on hers, his warmth giving her a sweet feeling. "I'm not worried about needing a home."

"I am." She wouldn't have him lost and homeless.

"How about a picnic once we get out of here?"

"Like a date?" Her eyebrows flew up, and her smile widened.

"Well, Barbara and Tracy would be there..."

"Oh, sorry." She tried to hurry and reel the smile back in and rewind her words. "I jumped ahead."

"But maybe..." Rigel grinned and gently squeezed her hand.

"Maybe..." Cori's smile returned. "Did you know that Rigel is the seventh brightest star in the night sky and the brightest in the Constellation of Orion?"

His hand remained in hers as they both stared up at the starless ceiling. "I didn't, but I did know it was a star."

"Cori stands for Corinth which was once one of the largest and most important cities in Greece. Definitely not as cool as being named after a star." She held her lips together to stop talking. "Sorry for rambling. I tend to talk about facts too much, which is probably why I have no real fans on my social media. And sometimes my facts are wrong."

"I don't mind, darlin', even though I have no idea what social media is."

Cori explained to him exactly what it was, but it would've been much easier to show him.

They then sat in silence until eventually Cori drifted off into a dream with her on a stage, playing a song—but she wasn't alone anymore.

Something tapped the space in between Cori's eyes and she woke on her back, with Lilith hovering over her. Lilith's nose rested millimeters from touching Cori's, and the demon's hot cinnamon breath tickled her lips.

"It's showtime," Lilith gasped. "Or should I just remove your heads and wait for the next person?"

The sound of rustling and a gun being messed with echoed. And then Cori's gaze met Rigel's as his rifle pointed at Lilith's head.

"Aww, the boy wants to be so brave." Lilith could do whatever she wanted, but she removed herself from Cori's body.

"What's going on?" Tracy asked with a yawn.

"Oh, just playing Cowboys and Indians," Lilith

answered and winked at Cori.

Strange.

Before the group left the safety of the sanctuary, they each retrieved an apple for breakfast and exited in a rush, hopefully to avoid a meet with the Devil. Cori never thought she would be saying something like that, but what a turn of events. At that moment, she wished she had her crochet hook as she walked, or her guitar, to keep from growing antsier. But nothing could save her from her anxiety, not in this hell-hole.

The forest was crowded with curving trees in full bloom and the creature sounds never faded. As they walked farther and farther, the world around her became darker. Lightning flashed through the fire sky, making the flames grow brighter. Fear flooded her veins and she knew that if something fell from the sky, that it wouldn't be rain—it would be scorching *fire*.

In the distance, tall flames the size of skyscrapers swayed. There would be no way to cross that, no matter how high she jumped. That was why Lilith was there, to perform whatever tricks were up her sleeve. A blackened desert came into view, and the group quickly started to cross it.

"What's going on, Rigel?" Barbara asked when their purple auras lit up. All except for Lilith's. Before anyone else noticed, charred fingertips pushed up from the ground. A protruding clawed hand swiped at her leg, and Cori leapt over it. They all made it across to the flames, so she thought. Barbara was still being too safe, but if Cori made it in her bulky boots, then Barbara should be fine. When a clawed hand reached out, tripping Barbara, Cori wanted to scream her name. However, she knew she couldn't yell and draw anyone or anything else's attention. It was too late—another clawed hand was already dragging the soul downward from Barbara's chest.

"Can't worry about that now," Lilith sang in Cori's ear. "Two gone, three left."

Somehow Tracy overheard and whispered, "You mean, one gone, four left."

"My mind is spinning in circles today." Lilith shook her head and shooed Cori and Rigel on. "You two need to hurry. I'll be here with Tracy."

Softly, Cori clawed at her own neck to show Lilith that if the demon tried anything, she'd rip her throat out with the pitchfork. Lilith did a motion back that she would be off with her head if Cori tried.

Cori couldn't worry about any of that right then. They needed to hurry while the Devil was hopefully at rest. With her hands together, she spread them out to pretend she was parting the flames, when really it was Lilith doing so.

The palace wasn't as she expected. The parted flames were the actual doors and the rest looked like molten rock stitched together to form a solid cube building.

Rigel slipped past the flaming entrance first, and she quickly caught up. With each step, beads of perspiration trickled down her body. The vinyl dress—she now wished she'd left at home—clung to her skin. She wanted to rip it off and just walk naked the remainder of the way, but she would still feel hot no matter what. If they didn't find this damn pitchfork, her skin would melt off soon.

They trekked through a large room that looked like the clusterfuck of all clusterfucks. At first she thought it was a study because of the old-timey desk and bookshelf, but then she spotted the bright red carpet with a black zigzag design, followed by arcade games, things that looked like they were from gladiator times, a record player, Greek statues, and more clutter. Up ahead—at the end of the room—on the wall sat the pitchfork, next to various weapons with sharp ends.

Rigel made the first move and lifted the pitchfork from the wall and handed it to Cori. She grabbed a knife next, so Tracy would have something since Rigel had his gun. Wrong move. Because that's when the ground shook.

Cori and Rigel both looked at each other and mouthed the word "run" at the same time. Gray apparitions formed around the room, swirling and churning, flying above her, below her, around her, through her. The spirits of the dead, of those who had been reaped for whatever the Devil did with them. No longer the beautiful soft purple, but the dull gray with no life attached.

The apparitions' mouths moved but nothing came out, not a sound, silenced forever and ever. Just like she would be silenced and burning forevermore if they didn't get the fuck out of there.

When they reached the exit out of the palace, the flames were once again closed. But the fire separated, like Moses moving apart the sea. But it wasn't Moses, it was only Lilith pretending to be, her lips drawn back into a snarl.

As Cori and Rigel burst through the open flames, Lilith growled, "What did you do?"

"We only grabbed the pitchfork and a knife," Cori rushed out the words.

Lilith snatched the knife from Cori's hand and threw it back inside. "I told you to grab the pitchfork!"

"But you said nothing else!"

"Too late now," Lilith groaned. "He's coming."

"You're not Deb, are you?" Tracy asked, her voice trembling.

Cori shook her head as they hauled ass back across the zombified desert and ran and ran past trees and berry bushes until they reached the shimmering canoe. Tracy jumped in first, followed by Lilith, Cori, and then Rigel. This time when the canoe made its passage, it didn't slowly barrel its way across. The boat skidded in a hurry as if motored by some type of engine, or more precisely powered by Lilith.

Moments later, the canoe came to a clunky stop, making Cori lurch forward. They hopped out from the boat and ran toward the spot where each of them had fallen through. Somehow, Cori or someone would need to push the pitchfork into the dirt to unlock the entrance. She didn't know if it would really work because it sounded dumb, but it was possibly their only chance.

A burst of flames circled the four of them and they halted again as everyone but Lilith shone a purple aura. A low growl and vicious roar—that Cori remembered all too clearly—sounded. Not a second too soon, two hellhounds with their demon riders stormed through the flames, fire mingling with their own orange glows.

"Calm down, boys," Lilith murmured, reaching out a hand.

One of the hellhounds snapped at her fingers, and Lilith pulled them back just before she lost the majority of her digits.

"When I'm in charge," Lilith barked, "you'll be dead and I'll eat you for dinner!"

Cori was pretty sure that all four of them were going

to be their dinner instead. Her gaze met Rigel's and they both now knew exactly what Lilith wanted. To be in charge. That was all fine and dandy, because Cori didn't care who was in charge, as long as they got the fuck out.

Lilith attempted to yank the weapon from Cori's hands, but as soon as it brushed the demon's fingertips, it burned her. "You're going to have to kill them," Lilith spat.

Kill a hellhound? Her? As one barreled for Cori, a bullet went off from Rigel's shotgun. She shoved the pitchfork into both the hellhound's eyes to kill him as Rigel had done the rider. The devil-horned demon slumped to the ground, and both rider and hellhound burst into flames. Rigel had no more bullets and Cori knew there was one hellhound carrying another rider somewhere around them.

"Behind you!" Lilith shouted, releasing flames from her hand to the rider.

"Why didn't you do that earlier?" Cori cried.

"Just testing your strength."

Cori wanted to jam the pitchfork into Lilith's face, too, but instead she thrust it into the hellhound's and pretended it was the demoness's skull.

As the flames died around them, a new cloud of fire drifted their way. With it came the Devil, who cascaded down in front of the group.

"What do we have here?" the Devil barked, curling the ends of his dark mustache. "*Lilith.*"

He did a strange movement with his hands as they crossed. Lilith stepped forward, her body alight in flames. She spun in a circular motion and the flames flew from her body and entered the Devil. He screamed and writhed in pain but also something else—pure anger.

"Stab him with the pitchfork!" Lilith demanded.

Cori stood there frozen, thinking too long about whether to trust Lilith or not. Tracy took the initiative and yanked it from Cori's hand, shoving it directly into the Devil's neck. Like the hellhounds and their riders, the Devil broke into flickering flames before vanishing to nothing. Lilith grasped the pitchfork from the dirt. Tracy smiled, then suddenly slumped to the ground, her purple soul ripped away from her body by Lilith.

Cori's eyes widened as her lips parted.

"You two look so surprised." Lilith shrugged. "I had to reap a soul after the Devil was gone to become the one in charge here. Would you rather it have been one of yours?"

Covering her mouth, Cori looked around the place and wanted to say yes, wanting to be that self-sacrificing type of person, but she didn't want to remain down there for all eternity. So she kept her mouth shut.

"You could have asked," Rigel said, still holding onto his now-empty gun.

"It isn't too late to have your soul reaped, if you so wish." Lilith rubbed the ends of the pitchfork. "Or do you want to go home?"

Closing his eyes, he sighed. "Home." Cori wished for that, too.

"That's what I thought." Lilith floated upward and rammed the pitchfork into the ceiling. Then she yanked the weapon out and shoved it into the ground once she came back down. A clanging noise stirred from above. The entrance rose … away from them, forming the long tunnel that Cori originally fell down from.

"There's no way we can climb up!" The hope within Cori withered away.

Lilith's pitchfork remained in the ground as she grabbed both of Cori's wrists tightly. "Thanks for being my little helper."

Cori ripped her wrists away and the ground under her and Rigel's feet rose upward.

"Rest in peace, sweetheart," Lilith called to Rigel.

Above the two of them, the dirt ceiling approached— Cori placed her hands in front of her face. A rumble sounded, and Cori relaxed as she peered through her fingers when the entrance reopened.

As the ground they stood on halted, Cori couldn't reach the ledge. Rigel lifted her and she crawled her way out onto snow-covered grass. When she turned around, Rigel was halfway out, but she latched onto his hands anyway and pulled him out from Hell.

High in the sky, the sun was already setting. What time was it? What day was it? No, what year was it? Cori scanned the yard—everything looked the same. Lots of trees, wooden patio furniture, two pink flamingos beside the rusted barbecue pit. But she still didn't know how much time had passed.

Cori turned to Rigel and swept her hand across the yard. "This is my home."

Rigel smiled as he took everything in. He opened his mouth to say something, but a cough escaped him.

"You alright?"

His cough turned into a rack of them. Charcoal gray dust spewed out of his mouth while his skin grew paler.

Cori didn't know what to do as she desperately searched around. She placed her shaky hands on his cool cheeks and stared at the ground for anything coming up to attack, but nothing happened. "What's wrong?"

"It was nice meeting you, darlin'," Rigel rasped. "I

should have known good things might come to an end.”

Cori thought about the year he fell in and how long had passed between then and now. “It’s the time, isn’t it? It’s catching up.”

He gave her a sullen nod. “We’ll have to delay that picnic for a bit. If there’s a Heaven, which I think there is after this, I’ll meet you in the clouds with two glasses of wine.”

“Lilith! Lilith!” Cori shouted, frantic, and she watched, with tears falling down her cheeks, Rigel’s body collapse to the ground. Ash stained her fingertips as he broke into too many small pieces to ever put back together.

Dropping to her knees on the grass, Cori slapped the ground. “You bitch!”

When no one answered, she glanced back at her house. How was she ever supposed to go back to her old life? How was she ever supposed to pretend that none of this had happened? A bad dream. That was what she would have to pretend it was.

The sun was already down as she dragged her feet toward the backdoor, finding it locked. She knocked, and all she could think about was Rigel’s ashes scattered around the yard. After a few more seconds, her brother tore open the door.

“Ryan,” she breathed without an ounce of strength left. He didn’t look older but there was a baby in his arms—her niece. The baby had been born while Cori was gone and appeared to be no more than six months. So she’d been gone possibly *seven* months.

Both her wrists itched and she scratched at them.

“Cori!” Ryan pulled her inside with one hand and held the baby in the other. “Where the hell have you been?"

"That is precisely the answer. I've been in Hell."

Questions were fired at her left and right from her parents, and she didn't know how to answer them. The police department was called, a psychiatrist would be called.

The new baby was named Phoebe, and she was cute, but Cori couldn't bring herself to hold her niece. She'd seen death, had made friends, lost friends, found the perfect guy, lost the perfect guy. Was now back here in this shithole, yet it was better than the other shithole.

For the next few nights, both her wrists continued to itch. When the sky darkened, Cori walked outside to stare up at the sky, looking for the star Rigel. She couldn't find it, but she knew it was out there somewhere.

"Cori," a voice whispered around her, distinctly familiar. She stared ahead at the ground, not seeing it move. "Cori," Lilith whispered again, "get the baby." Where her wrists itched, fluorescent symbols of snakes took shape—the places Lilith had touched her.

Thanks for being my little helper.

Lilith had meant in the future, not the past, just as she'd told Rigel to rest in peace. Cori-couldn't stop the urge burgeoning inside her, needing to get the baby. The baby she *needed* to bring to Lilith—and many more babies after that.

Cori was still herself, and she knew it was wrong, but she couldn't control it.

She'd seen the movie *Labyrinth* one too many times, and she always thought she would be like the character Sarah, but instead, she was now like one of the goblins, and Lilith was not her Goblin Queen, but her Demon Queen.

Thorna

*T*horna sat in her throne, peering up at the dancing butterflies, interweaving through the thorn branches. To the humans, she and her beasties would either be considered gods or monsters, and perhaps both were true. She did kill and drink the blood of pixies when they bothered her beasties, but those creatures were pests, villainous in her world. Most of the stories in the mortal world about fae were untrue—she didn't like to toy with humans. *Much.* She had found the majority of them rather dull. Until Asher.

"That … that ending," Pyrka said, peering up at her, his dark lips parted.

"Yes?" Thorna grinned.

"I want to know more."

Thorna had penned a second set of the stories to give one to Pyrka each day. But she would have him read them the following day because she didn't want him to make her rethink sending something if he hated one. What was done was done. Yet she had to share them with someone.

"Then you can use your imagination, Pyrka." Thorna grinned and patted his cheek. "Feed the butterflies pixie blood—they are thirsty. I shall be back soon."

"Yes, my queen." Pyrka bowed and lifted a bucket full of blood beside the water wall.

With a wave of her hand, she shifted to moth and dove straight through the liquid, entering the mortal world. The wind pierced her fragile body, stronger than the prior night. She fluttered her emerald wings harder, inhaling the scents of woods and chemical pollution, until she arrived on Asher's lamp-lit street. Same as the night before, she peered into his window, discovering him reading something. Her story…

With a smile and her heart galloping, Thorna shifted into her fae form. Her leather pants hugged her legs tighter as she knelt to retrieve the next scroll and thorned twig. She placed them both on the doorstep, rang the bell, then disappeared back into the darkness. A part of her yearned to steal Asher away to her kingdom, but she fought to keep her hands to herself.

Thorna hadn't planned on coming back the next day to the antique shop, but she did. The day before, she had bought two teacups. And when she had smelled both, the memories of the previous owners had rushed through her. That was what she liked the most about antiques, knowing the memories the objects held. Whether beautiful, hateful, melancholic—she wanted to see and feel what others had in the past.

"You're back." The man smiled, tapping his fingers along the desk as he circled around it to approach her. He wore a button-up shirt over a horror movie tee and tight jeans that showed off his lean legs.

"I suppose I am." Thorna inched closer, tugging at the hem of the T-shirt she wore. She couldn't wear her clothing from home if she wanted to blend in, but she still left her hair emerald. So many mortals colored their hair

these days compared to the past when she had needed to change it.

"I'm Asher, by the way." It was a kingly name, one that somehow matched him well.

"Thorna." She glanced up at the glass cabinet in front of her. "Are you getting more teacups in?"

"Thorna," he said softly, as though tasting her name. "Tell me what you're looking for, and I'll make sure to find it for you."

Her heart swelled, knowing he would search for any object she so desired.

Inside the Box

$\mathcal{M}$aggie had been hidden away inside this box for what seemed like eons and eons, but it must have been closer to seven months since her stomach was stretched and swollen as far as it could possibly get.

The darkness covered her with a cool blanket for most of the hours that ticked away inside her skull.

A door slowly creaked open from outside her prison walls, causing Maggie's heart to still, or as much stilling as a heart could do.

Maggie lifted her hands and placed them against her stomach, protecting what was inside from being taken by *her*.

The dreaded sounds of familiar footsteps, and the rattling of her food tray, reverberated around her as Mother approached. Maggie's stomach growled in betrayal. The steps drifted closer and closer, being absorbed by the space in this coffin—her tomb.

Clanging radiated as Mother set the food tray somewhere near Maggie, and several seconds of bolts being released echoed in her ears. *Click, click, click— creakkkkk.* The dark door opened above Maggie. A candescent light filtered throughout the room, and her eyes tried to adjust. Maggie blinked several times before her gaze focused on golden hair pulled into a high bun.

Maggie knew she wouldn't be able to escape—she'd tried—multiple times. Mother had easily put a stop to that.

Body trembling, Maggie brought herself to a sitting position as the jangling from her chained ankles vibrated against the metal cuffs encircling her skin, rubbed raw after so many months. Her wrists were just as sore from the handcuffs binding them together.

"How are you, baby?" Mother whispered softly as though she was talking to an infant instead of a fully grown woman.

"Mother, please, I can't handle this anymore. Why are you doing this to me? What are you going to do to the baby?" Maggie peered down at her stomach, trying to solve the endless riddle. Greasy blonde locks of hair swung forward, touching her lips. She let out a huff of air and shoved them away. The red dress she wore was now covered in grime and holes, a putrid smell hitting her nose.

Inside the box, Maggie had wondered what Mother was going to do to the baby once he or she arrived. Mother was never like this before, not until she found out Maggie was pregnant with James's baby. The day replayed like an old vinyl record, skipping and echoing.

"Mother, I'm pregnant." Maggie's heart constricted tighter than a dried-up fruit. She knew Mother would be disappointed. Mother had only met James once, then forbade Maggie to ever see him again. Maggie was already eighteen, but didn't have a job that would allow her to leave home, and she hadn't known James for that long. But when she fell for him, she fell fast, and she fell hard.

"With that man's baby?" Mother screeched and slapped the wall so hard a few of the pictures twisted to the side in a crooked dance.

He was twenty-eight, and maybe that was Mother's problem, but it wasn't Maggie's. "Yes, his baby. Who else's baby would it be?"

"Obviously, it could be anyone's now that I know I raised a harlot who sleeps with evil," Mother spat and slapped the wall harder. This time a picture slid down the wall and crashed along the floor. Glass broke and shattered into a mixture of large and tiny pieces.

"I'm going to tell him now, but I wanted you to know first." Maggie turned around without uttering another word, her red dress swishing.

It would take some time for Mother—Maggie too.

Mother didn't follow Maggie to her room as she went to gather a few things for their dinner tonight. Maybe James would let Maggie move in with him. If not, she needed to figure things out on her own.

Maggie walked to the closet and collected a weekend's worth of clothing and stuffed it all into her backpack before she sat heavily on the bed with a sigh. "How could I have let this happen?" she whispered. Tears slid down her face, and she felt like screaming.

The shuffle of footsteps sounded behind her. Without turning around, Maggie said, "I know, Mother. When I get back, I'll sit down and talk about it with you."

Something soft and wet pressed against Maggie's nose and mouth, causing her to struggle to breathe. Choking, Maggie tried to break away from the cloth, but black dots pulled at the edges of her eyes until she collapsed.

Maggie's eyelids fluttered open for a second, then she was yanked back down to the blackened pit. With all the strength she could muster, Maggie attempted to lift her eyelids open again, only to catch a blurry glimpse of golden hair, blue eyes, and a straight nose.

"Mother?" Maggie gasped. She moved to push herself off the floor, but her wrists were bound together by something. Handcuffs.

"You're all right, Maggie. You're safe now." Mother walked toward Maggie and gripped her shoulders to tug her into a sitting position on her knees.

The woman had gone mad. Maggie's mother had always been strict, but this was different. As her heartbeat quickened, something told her that she needed to escape.

Maggie's gaze flicked from left to right, taking in the poorly-lit room and the turquoise-painted walls. In the center rested an obsidian, rectangular box, the size and shape of a coffin. She had never seen this place before. The room slowly stopped spinning, and Maggie tried to swallow, finding instead that her throat was dry. "Where am I?"

Mother's hazel eyes narrowed at Maggie, and she shuddered. "I said you were safe. You're safe here from him." She ran a hand over her bun. "You, dear child, aren't going anywhere."

Rubbing the insides of her wrists, Maggie was unable to squeeze out from the cuffs. "How long are you planning to keep me here?"

Mother reached behind her back, drawing out a tan ruler. Before Maggie could speak, Mother slammed the wood against her knuckles. Maggie yelped as pain coursed through her fingers. The ruler slapped her knuckles once more.

Mother ran the wood across her palm. "I've already answered that question, Maggie."

Maggie held her breath, wishing for the ache in her hands to cease.

"You brought him here!" Mother screamed, cracking the ruler to her thigh at the same time.

Maggie's tongue felt thick in her mouth. "I—I don't know what you're talking about," she stuttered, praying that the ruler wouldn't come down on her knuckles again.

Mother took a step closer toward her. "The man with the ship. Who else?"

"Ship?" Maggie furrowed her brow, confusion encircling her. "Man?"

Mother reached out and gripped the collar of Maggie's dress. Beads of perspiration coated Mother's forehead. "The seed! The seed! You're carrying his blasted seed."

"What are you talking about?" Maggie bit back.

"His child!"

"James? You're talking about James. He doesn't have a ship!" she shouted in Mother's face.

"I'm going to have to tuck you away until we can hide the child. Get in the box now!"

Maggie's gaze angled toward the dark object. "I'm not getting in there."

Mother grabbed Maggie by the arms, her nails digging crescent moons into her flesh. Maggie's heart pounded against her sternum as she grew panicked.

Hoping to hit Mother in the face, Maggie threw her head forward. The contact caused pain to ripple through Maggie as Mother drew in a sharp breath. She hurried to stand, desperately needing to leave the room, but her feet lost purchase, her balance gone when Mother's hands clamped down on her arms. Maggie's back hit the hard surface inside the box, the air leaving her lungs. She lay dazed, helpless, as the heavy lid slammed shut.

Now, Mother stood before her, appearing as if she hadn't eaten in weeks with her sunken cheeks and purple bags beneath her eyes. "We have to get the baby away. I've told you that." Her voice was frantic.

"You're mad and—" A sharp ache swarmed in Maggie's stomach, her knees buckling, and she collapsed against the cement flooring.

Mother's eyes widened and she knelt beside Maggie. "The baby is coming, and we have to hurry before he arrives. Lay on your back."

Maggie didn't answer when the pain increased, only did as she was asked. Mother spread Maggie's knees apart and hiked up her dress above her waist. Heavy breaths escaped Maggie's lips as a warm liquid pooled out from between her legs.

Tightening her fists, Maggie clenched her teeth and fought back the waves of agony pulsing through her abdomen and lower back. Mother attempted to calm Maggie's nerves by rubbing her knees, and she couldn't find the energy to shove her away.

"Push," Mother shouted, clenching one of Maggie's thighs.

For once, Maggie listened. Pushing and screaming and pushing again and again, the room growing smaller and smaller around her. She didn't know how much time had passed when, finally, a loud wail filled the air, bouncing off the walls.

"It's a boy." Mother sighed in relief, bringing the red-faced infant up to Maggie. He was a wrinkled thing with a button nose and pale hair atop his head.

"Peter," Maggie whispered, chest heaving.

A heavy noise rumbled from somewhere outside the room, then what sounded like a shattering of glass. Maggie froze.

Mother's eyes widened and her lips parted as she focused on Maggie and asked, "You or the baby?"

"*What?*" What the hell kind of question was that? And why would she even need to make that choice?

"Who would you save?" Mother's gaze darted between Maggie and the closed door. "I can't save you both."

Maggie knew Mother needed help, and to keep Peter safe for now, she would choose. A fear swarmed over her, one that festered within her thoughts of Mother hurting the baby. "Peter."

Mother kissed her forehead with tenderness. "I love you, Maggie. You'll understand why I did this when he gets here." Without another word, Mother rushed out of the room, cradling Peter tightly in her arms.

Maggie lifted herself on her forearms, exhaustion consuming her as she pushed herself up to stand, the chains and handcuffs still intact. The door stood wide open, and Maggie hobbled toward the exit to chase after Mother. Blood streamed down her thighs, the chains clanking with each step.

She reached the doorway—only to crash into a hard chest. Maggie stumbled back to look up at a bearded face, chestnut eyes, dark hair swept back. He wore a red and black cloak that fell to his knees, and she saw at the end of its right sleeve, not a hand but a silver hook. It took her a second to recognize the man.

"James?" she rasped.

"Maggie, where's your mother?" His tone was straight and to the point, no surprise in seeing her for the first time in months.

"She took the baby, *our* baby, James." Maggie's gaze shot wildly down the empty, narrow hallway.

"It took me a while to realize it was *her*," James growled, a deep scowl settling on his handsome face. "Then when you two disappeared, it all came to me. You know, your mother and I have a history together. In a place called Neverland."

Maggie's eyes widened, and nausea filled her stomach.

James lifted his hand and slid his index finger across her lower lip. "Don't give me that look. Tinker and I never once had relations like you and I did, my beauty."

"James?" Maggie's voice trembled.

"I know all about the prophecy, and I will find our precious Peter Pan." He paused. "And he will die."

Maggie's words turned to concrete in her throat. She couldn't wrap her mind around what he'd said.

"How do you know the baby's name?" she finally managed to get out.

He didn't answer, only gripped her upper arms, and she couldn't escape his grasp. James lifted her and walked toward the middle of the room while she twisted and kicked, but her muscles were too weak after giving birth. As he reached the box, James dropped her inside. Maggie gasped from the sharp pain radiating up her spine.

"This is full of maps of the place where I'm returning on my ship." He lifted something from his back pocket— a book—and tossed it inside with her before slamming the lid. "But I don't think you'll be able to catch up."

Maggie screamed, venom in her voice. "Let me out, you mother fucker!" Strength came back to her as she twisted and thrust her body within the confines of the box, but the lid didn't move a single inch. There was a *click-click-click.* Each bolt being locked.

"Enjoy your rest, my beauty," James crooned.

The sound of his footsteps faded away, and Maggie continued to bang and bang against the lid until her fists were raw, her voice hoarse.

A sinking feeling washed over Maggie when smoke enveloped her, stinging her eyes. Her breaths started to come in short gasps as her lungs screamed in protest. The temperature within the box rose, and Maggie knew she would never leave again.

She waited for blistering, searing flames to cook her flesh and lick the skin from her bones. But Maggie knew in her heart that she'd made the right choice in saving Peter.

Thorna

*T*horna sipped on pixie blood while watching Pyrka scan over her story.

He peered up at her, eyes wide. "I think burning would be a terrible way to die, yet I loved the story."

"I agree, but there are worse ways to die." She arched a brow and imagined all the possible ways as he rested her pages on the table beside the throne.

These stories, they were her words, her feelings. Dark at times, lovely at times.

A black and white butterfly landed on her fingertip. "You're thirsty, aren't you?" Thorna placed the butterfly on the edge of the bucket filled with pixie blood. She watched a swarm of butterflies interweave around one another as they ventured to sate their appetites.

"See you soon, Pyrka," Thorna said before transforming to a moth and darting toward Asher's home.

The black sky concealed the world, the flickering stars guiding her way to Asher's neighborhood.

On his door, a note written on printing paper was taped to it. *How about waiting for me to answer after ringing the doorbell this time?* Thorna's heart pounded, brutally, as she transformed. She shakily retrieved the scroll and thorns from her satchel, yearning to stay and show herself. But she wouldn't. She wanted to give him this part of herself, do something for him, the way he had for her these past few months.

Ringing the doorbell, she shifted into her moth form and soared off down the street, not even chancing a glance through Asher's window. Because then she knew she would give in and take him away.

"Do you live around here?" Asher asked. "You've been coming in every day for the past couple of weeks."

"Sometimes." She smiled.

Asher arched a brow. "Well, that means on those 'sometimes,' you can continue coming in."

"If you keep bringing in new antiques each day, then yes." But she knew that wasn't the only reason.

"I'll get right on that." He chuckled. "I really like the color of your hair."

Most mortals tried to touch her emerald locks when they told her this, then she had to toy with them. But not Asher—he hadn't attempted to touch her. Yet she wanted to feel his long fingers wrapped in her hair.

The Celebration Game

Bronwyn stroked the letter over and over with a smile. Adrian had given it to her a few nights ago before he left, and he just knew how to tickle her fancy. Today was the day—Mardi Gras—their yearly event.

The oven beeped, and she set the letter on the table beside Adrian's other gift. She strolled to the stove and opened the door to a rush of heat. The king cake looked perfect with the right amount of brown coloring, not too dark, not too light—it would be quite an image.

After setting it down to cool, Bronwyn figured she had waited long enough to open the box that had accompanied Adrian's note. Inside rested a green Mardi Gras mask with purple and gold feathers rising from the center in between the eyes. She took out the next gift—a dress of green silk, adorned with pearl buttons down the center, that fell just above the knees. Two secret pockets were hidden along the sides. She *loved* pockets.

She, Adrian, and their seven friends would be playing an annual game in a matter of hours, and her fingers tapped her lip in anticipation. Last year, Adrian had won the escape room game—but Bronwyn vowed that it would be her this year.

It was more fun than any game she'd ever played, better than Clue or Monopoly, because only the nine of them participated and no one else.

Bronwyn hummed under her breath as she gathered the decorations for the king cake. Her heart wanted to burst with excitement over the small gift she'd baked inside for Adrian.

When the clock struck six, she was already dressed and ready to go downtown. The mask she chose to set on top of the cake box, which was itself piled atop the special dish. As part of their tradition, each of her friends had to bring one. Picking up the whole lot, she walked to the car and loaded the goodies inside.

Most would pick Christmas or possibly Halloween as their favorite day of the year, but hers was the first day of Mardi Gras. It was the one night where she truly felt free.

While Bronwyn drove downtown, she stared at the buildings. New Orleans had a special architecture, and a lovely and eccentric group of people. There were the superstitions such as the roots in Voodoo and the famous voodoo queen, Marie Laveau, then there was the history that held so much emotion, the traditions—such as Mardi Gras. The diversity and the creativity here, she felt that no other place quite matched up. Watching people eat beignets from Café du Monde was one of her favorite pastimes. The one downfall to the city was sometimes the unpleasant smells in certain parts—urine, too many cigarettes, and vomit.

It was still early, but not too early for drunks. Two drivers had already swerved in front of her as she passed them, and another nearly crashed into her car. She hated driving, rarely ever did it.

As she turned down a couple of streets, the Mardi Gras floats slipped into view. They were always strange, a wonderful kind of weird. One appeared to be a bright emerald dragon, sprouting wings of gold and violet, with an even darker tongue of purple poking out. Another was a woman, almost sea nymph-like—lavender and gold flowers woven in her yellow hair as she pressed her lips to a crimson flute. Bronwyn caught the third before moving on to the next street—a laughing jester wearing a blue hat with silver jingle bells. It held out something similar to a rattle, the top resembling a baby jester head.

Bronwyn knew locals were tossing plastic beads, toys, candy, and more to the tourists, who acted as if they were catching gold. Perhaps it was better than gold to them, at least for these few days.

She drew closer to a street sign, announcing the location of the escape room. Bronwyn took a left and parked the car on the side near the curb, then dropped a few coins into the parking meter. Opening the passenger side door, she placed the feathered mask over her face and grabbed the cake box and the covered silver dish.

The buildings on this side of the street were mostly abandoned, so only a few people passed her as she walked up to the front door. The smell of piss permeated the air and she wrinkled her nose in disgust—it always reeked of the foul odor in this area.

Background noises tickled her ears—a cheering in the distance, the rumbles of the floats moving. A red door, with chipped paint and the number 204 scrawled in black marker, greeted her. On the entrance hung a large, vibrant wreath decorated in purple and white plaid ribbons linked with other gold and green mesh. In the middle lay a plastic baby, about the size of a newborn.

Bronwyn had never understood the point of the baby. Yes, he was meant to represent the baby Jesus and how he first entered the world, but why stuff him in cake and plaster him on other things? Curious, indeed. She held Adrian's cake closer to her chest, already anticipating his expression when the clock struck midnight.

Careful not to drop the food, Bronwyn gave a shallow knock at the door, then tapped the melody that only Adrian and their friends knew.

The door swung open, and there stood Adrian. The hazel eyes behind his disguise complimented his warm brown skin and wavy black hair. A mask similar to hers hid the top portion of his face, except his was covered in gold and white feathers. Her gaze drifted to his purple button-up shirt, black vest, and slacks, then ventured back up to his face.

Everyone generally put their masks on at the stroke of midnight to celebrate the occasion, but Adrian and Bronwyn always came early to reveal themselves to each other before the others joined.

"I baked a surprise inside the cake for you," Bronwyn said as she stepped into the room. "But you'll have to wait until midnight to retrieve it."

Adrian rubbed his hands together as he peered down at the cake. "Can't wait."

Balloons filled the room across the ceiling. Streamers intertwined against the rail of both staircases leading to the second floor. Ceramic masks with painted faces hung on the walls, and colorful paper squares were scattered on the tile.

The main area sat empty except for a long oval table in the center, surrounded by nine chairs. A green cloth lay draped over the table, and a diamond-shaped purple and gold runner was pushed across. From the ceiling dangled a Mardi Gras beaded chandelier.

"Wow. Simon really outdid himself this year." Bronwyn headed toward the dining area.

"He says he needs to outdo himself every year."

"Well, he certainly did," she said, placing the food items on the table beside another silver covered dish that Adrian had brought.

Adrian leaned over her, caging her in. "My, my." He grinned while peering down at her hands. "I didn't know you could cook."

"I just followed the instructions." Bronwyn's voice came out breathy as he pressed his nose into the crook of her neck. Her heart fluttered at the sensual touch. "I thought you said in the note I'd have to wait until midnight for a kiss." She tilted her head farther to the right, allowing him better access. "Or two."

"Who said anything about kissing just yet?" With gentle hands, Adrian slowly removed the mask from her face and tossed it to the table.

Bronwyn whirled around and caged Adrian, this time, against the wall. Almost as gingerly as he had, she took the mask from his face, and inspected the curve of his jaw, the high cheekbones, the shallow lines at the edges of his eyes. Her gaze locked onto his hazel irises—her favorite part of him.

"You're always beautiful," Adrian whispered. Before she could return the compliment, he grabbed her by the waist and easily hoisted her up, his mask falling from her hand. Letting out an anxious sound, Bronwyn wrapped her legs around his sturdy torso.

Adrian caressed a tendril of her dark brown hair

around his fingertip. "We have plenty of time until the others get here."

Bronwyn inspected the room, which was lacking any sort of soft furniture. "As usual, there's not a bed."

"But there are the stairs," he murmured in her ear.

She brushed her middle finger across his plump lower lip. "Or the floor."

"Or the table."

The table was a perfect idea. She reached for the buttons at the front of her silk dress and undid one at a time while he held her up, finally exposing her full breasts. Adrian groaned low as he lowered her body on top of the table.

"Just watch out for the cake," she purred as he unzipped his pants, then pressed his weight on top of her. Adrian's hand cradled her breast, his thumb stroking her hard nipple. She moaned as his fingers drifted to between her thighs. With a sexy grin, he captured her mouth in a fierce kiss.

They then had their way with each other not only on the table, but also against the wall near the stairs, where the eyeless masks were their only audience.

The coded knock came right after they had straightened themselves out. It had already grown dark outside when they opened the door, and a clock indicated it was already after ten. Quinn and Theo arrived first. Quinn's hair was pulled up into a high ponytail, and Theo had put gold glitter into his dark beard. Next came Owen, then Aggie, and finally Hollis, Yan, and Simon.

All of them had known each other since they were young. Their town had been small, so they'd learned to lean on one another and make do.

Simon and Yan were the last to set their silver platters

on the table.

"Why does it smell like sex in here?" Yan asked, pushing a dark lock of her bobbed hair behind her ear.

Adrian exchanged a glance with Bronwyn, his smirk mirroring hers.

Simon let out a loud groan. "Just please tell me you two didn't exchange fluids on the table … again."

Bronwyn didn't answer, but let out a low whistle and focused her gaze on the beaded chandelier.

"Oh, they did!" Aggie scrunched up her small nose.

"I won't deny it," Adrian finally said.

"On to more important matters." Simon withdrew a piece of paper from the pocket of his jacket and placed it on the table so everyone could see. "These are the rules. As always, you'll split into pairs, which makes four groups. I'll be down here and all doors will remain locked until 11:45."

"Besides the room you start in, you'll have to cross through four others. The final door leading to the other set of stairs is your exit."

"Agreed," everyone said simultaneously.

"Now." Simon slid his bag across the table and opened it. "You will each get a flashlight. Make sure to keep hold of it, or things may become too difficult."

"Wow," Owen chimed in. "You really sound like you should do this professionally."

"Perhaps I should." Simon shoved a flashlight at Owen's chest. "Don't drop it."

He handed one to Hollis and she flicked it on and off, verifying it worked, then the rest of the group did the same. This little beam of light was the only tool they would have to start—no one could have cell phones or any other personal items for the hour they would have to play. It was the perfect tradition.

"Ready?" Yan asked, an anxious grin on her face as she took her first step on the staircase.

"Just hold your horses," Simon said, pushing himself to the front of the line. "Now, let's go."

Bronwyn followed behind Yan, with Adrian right at her back while they ascended the spiral staircase. There were no windows, and everything had been sealed up and soundproofed. If they desired to, they could shout as loud as they wanted without the police being called.

Adrian and Bronwyn had shouted one another's names during their earlier romp to see who could outdo the other—she'd won.

The two main exits of the building were both located on the first floor: one in the front, and the other in the back. Both were now locked, and Simon held the device to unseal all the doors.

At the top of the stairs, purple, gold, and green streamers lined the ceiling. Small plastic babies, Mardi Gras coins, and feathers were pasted to the walls.

"Seriously, how long did you spend getting these tiny coins on the wall?" Owen asked, his expression incredulous.

From everything Bronwyn was seeing, it must have taken a long while.

"A bit." Simon ran a finger across two of the coins.

"You need to get a good fuck," Owen said.

Simon arched a brow at Owen. "Are you offering?"

Bronwyn pressed a hand at her temple and ignored the on-and-off lovers' quarrel between Owen and Simon. She assumed they were off by the way Simon shot him the finger over something.

Adrian curled his arm around Bronwyn's waist and

whispered against her ear. "Are you scared?"

"No"—she relaxed her back against his chest—"are you?"

"Yeah." He chuckled. "Scared you'll win this year."

She smirked and gave him a soft shove. "If I win, I know exactly what I'm going to have you do."

Just as Adrian was going to respond, Simon asked, "Ready?"

Four doors painted half purple and half green opened via the gadget in Simon's hands. Hollis and Yan stepped through the first door, then Quinn and Owen into the next room, followed by Aggie and Theo, and finally Adrian and Bronwyn went into the last.

"Wait for the flashing light," Simon said, "because I'll be watching you if you cheat. See you all in about an hour. On the count of three. One, two, three." And the heavy doors shut, giving a soft rumble throughout the second floor, the locks clicking into place.

The room they started in was small. Purple and gold diamonds covered the walls, and a row of wooden panels accented the lower half. The only other thing besides the door across from them was a metal box hanging next to a ticking clock. Five minutes remained before the game would start.

"So." Adrian leaned against the wall, his arms crossed and his wavy hair brushing his eyebrows. "What do you want to talk about for the next five minutes?"

"You tell me." Bronwyn smiled, already plotting her first move—for the metal box.

Kicking off from the wall, he sauntered toward her and clasped her hand. He brought her inner wrist to his lips, his hazel eyes never leaving hers. "How about after tonight, we fly across the world?"

"Iceland." Bronwyn lifted their hands and twirled Adrian in a circle. A deep chuckle escaped his mouth.

"Then Russia." He gave her a bow.

She curtsied in return and thought of tea. "Then Japan."

"Then Antarctica."

She shivered at the thought and smiled at him. "Too cold."

"Ah, my beautiful hellion, a little cold never hurt anyone."

She'd traveled to lots of places. Alaska during the dead of winter had been one of the worst times in her life. "How about Egypt instead?"

"Pyramids? I like that." He twisted a lock of her hair around his finger. "I also like the new color. I should have mentioned that earlier."

She grasped his dark curls, interlacing them between her digits, so soft. "I like—"

A bang struck the wall, making them both jump, her forward and him backward. Adrian's hands tightened at her waist. When a loud moan sounded through the wall from the opposite side, they both laughed. Aggie and Theo.

"I always knew they would give in to temptation," Bronwyn said.

Aggie had given Theo secret looks while growing up. Bronwyn always noticed and had even told Aggie to make her move, but she had said she didn't feel like that for him. Even when Bronwyn had picked up on an answering interest in Theo for Aggie, still nothing happened—until now.

Adrian propped his hand against the wall. "I do remember it taking you quite some time to notice me."

He grinned, almost wolfishly. "Now I can't get you off of me."

Rolling her eyes, Bronwyn flicked her gaze at the clock. The red ticking hand beat its own drum as it moved upward. Seven. Six. Five. Four. Three. Two. One. A low *beep beep* came from the ceiling above, and the bulbs pulsed and flickered. Bronwyn closed her eyes, then blinked several times, finding it hard to focus on the dim light that barely brightened up anything.

"Teamwork, for now," she said when her head cleared, turning on her flashlight. "Let's go."

"Adjusting to the new light is a bitch." Adrian rubbed his eyes and shifted toward one of the wall panels.

The exit out of the room was the door in front of her, and she needed a key. That was the first thing they had to find. Adrian removed a panel and set it aside.

Bronwyn went for the metal box next to the clock. When she pulled on the knob, the door of the box creaked open. Inside rested something black. She pulled the dark object out then pressed the silver button, and a blade popped out. A switchblade. She was certain she would have to use it later for something, so she tucked it into the side pocket of her dress. Adrian hadn't seemed to be paying attention to the slip of the weapon, and she would keep that to herself. It was a competition, after all.

The other object was a silver key. She already knew it would be too predictable to have the key to their own door out, but she moved to try and unlock it anyway. No luck. It wouldn't even slide in.

"A-ha!" Adrian turned around with a grin, holding the wooden panel he'd just lifted from the wall. Behind it rested a set of metal chains covered in at least six keys and locks with jester faces painted on them.

Bronwyn watched as Adrian struggled with each key, trying to get them to fit the locks. Her impatience boiled until she realized none of them would fit, except for possibly the one in her hand. She knelt beside him and shined her flashlight on a lock. "Look." She held up the key and moved it to a lock that didn't budge, and neither did the next. On the third try, the lock gave. Quickly, she unraveled the chain and grabbed the key attached.

Bronwyn pulled the chain up and unlocked the next lock. Then she grabbed the newly-loosened chain with a key attached—strung in a crisscross pattern—before undoing another. She continued the movements until they were all opened except for the final small box in the middle. Finally, the bottom key was able to reach it, and she opened the box. It contained a plastic baby, and in its pudgy little hands sat a bronze key.

With a huge smile on her face, Bronwyn snapped up the key and tossed it in the air. Adrian swiped the key before it landed back into her palm.

"Let's hurry," he said, swiftly moving for the door.

As they reached the exit, a loud bang and crash came from the room beside theirs. Then something akin to a growl sounded, making Bronwyn's blood run cold. She stood frozen, and Adrian hadn't moved either.

"I don't think that's them having sex," Adrian said with wide eyes, hurrying to shove the key into the lock.

"It sounds wilder than even animal sex," she rushed out. "We need to see what's going on!"

"Simon!" Adrian yelled as he opened the door.

"Simon!" she echoed. He was the one who was watching them on the cameras.

Another intense growl stirred from next door, one that didn't sound anything like a human. A boisterous clatter reverberated through the shared wall of their rooms.

What was going on?

Adrian grabbed Bronwyn's wrist and pulled her through the door into another dimly-lit room. His brow furrowed as he stared at the wall and held onto the knob.

More beating came through the wall. Bang. Bang. *Bang!*

"What the fuck?" Bronwyn shouted as she grabbed the key from the lock.

Her heart kicked up a notch. She didn't know what was going on in her friends' room, but she had to get to them. Quickly, she ignored the locked exit ahead and shined the light to the door that would be Aggie and Theo's room. It was the only one of their friends' doors connected to their new challenge room at the moment. She wished the others had been joined to it as well, so she could see if they were okay.

"Stay as quiet as possible," Adrian said when he moved to their friends' door to unlock it from the twist bolt.

Bronwyn nodded and reached for the switchblade in her pocket.

Slowly, he opened the door. It creaked softly, but he continued to pull. Her gaze scanned the room, finally settling on two bodies covered in bright red. Aggie's blonde pixie cut was mussed, her throat torn open. The other body—Theo's—looked as if it had been ripped apart. There was blood splattered everywhere, the overwhelming metal odor invaded her nose.

Bronwyn covered her mouth with a trembling hand and followed Adrian's gaze up to a large hole rooted in the ceiling. A rustling and swishing noise echoed from inside it. Bronwyn thrust Adrian out of the way and shut the door, locking it. Something had made that hole in the ceiling, something that could very well come back down.

"We have to get out of here, *really* get out of here," she said, her breaths coming out too heavy. She felt as if she could hardly draw air into her panicked lungs.

"Right now, it looks like our options are that open hole or to find the code out of this room."

"I don't think going through that hole is the idea."

"What the hell happened in there?" Adrian asked, running his hands through his wavy hair.

Something had killed Aggie and Theo. Her friends' bodies were a mangled mess, and Bronwyn wanted to scream, wanted to cry, wanted to rage on whatever had done that. But whatever it was couldn't have been human. Not even a chainsaw would have mauled someone up like that, and what they had heard was not a tool of any kind. It was something distinctly more than human—more like an animal.

"I don't know," Bronwyn started. "but let's just focus on getting to the next room so we can find everyone else. I think waiting in this room for the doors to unlock wouldn't be an option right now. And where the hell is Simon?"

"I agree, but if something came through the ceiling of that room, do you think…"

She knew what he was thinking—that Simon could be dead.

Bronwyn was startled out of her thoughts by a booming crash. She glanced around, her heart pounding, but it sounded like the noise was coming from further away—possibly Owen and Quinn's room. But their room wasn't connected to this challenge room. Bronwyn and

Adrian needed to hurry.

Pointing her flashlight around the room, she noticed a small desk in the corner. A golden crown rested on top, surrounded by various bead necklaces, all the colors of Mardi Gras. Along the floor, board games were sprawled with their lids taken off.

The touchscreen lock on the exit door needed four numbers. Adrian started digging through the boxes, while Bronwyn headed for the desk. There were eight drawers and most sat empty except for one holding two flashlights. When she flicked the button up, a bluish UV light shot out. *Bingo*.

She handed one to Adrian as she scanned the room, searching for any sign of a code. All she could focus on was the constant beat of her heart and her heavy breathing.

A thunderous smack struck the door from Aggie and Theo's room. Bronwyn stood frozen for a second before moving faster. The beating against the door came harder and harder, and she was finding it difficult to concentrate on anything except that sound.

"We got this. Just try and drown it out," Adrian said as his hands shook and he angled his light against a box of a board game.

When another bang crashed, not against the door of Aggie and Theo's room, but somewhere inside where Bronwyn and Adrian had started, she realized they had both been idiots for leaving it open.

"Shut the fucking door!" Bronwyn screamed. She was too far away, but so was Adrian. As fast as she could, she ran to the opening and went to close it, yet her eyes briefly caught something. It rose from the wood floor and barreled to the door, pushing against her weight. Adrian lunged forward and slammed it closed, then scrambled to lock it.

The banging now erupted against the door, but all Bronwyn could think about was the face—that *thing*. She wanted to cover her ears, her eyes.

"Did you see it?" she whispered, her face going pale.

"Barely," he said. "A deep gray color."

"It had wings, Adrian, *wings*! And two horns, like a fucking demon from Hell."

"I believe you." His voice was firm, his breaths heavy.

But how was this possible?

Gathering whatever focus she could, Bronwyn glided the flashlight over the game boxes, and halted when one showed a hidden number behind the lid. 5316.

Adrian caught a glimpse of the code and rushed alongside her to enter the number. With hurried motions, she fingered in the numbers to the code and grasped the lid in her other hand, not risking leaving it behind. *Access Granted.* The metal door cracked open and after they entered, she pulled it closed behind them.

Bronwyn tossed the box lid to the floor—they were supposed to leave the code for the next group that needed it, but they were both dead. *Dead.* She couldn't bring herself to think about that word. Not now.

There were two other metal doors in the new challenge room besides the outlet from which she and Adrian came out of: one that led to the next exit and the other from which her four remaining friends would be coming in. That was, if they did, or perhaps they already had. But there was no way to open her friends' door from this side like they had with Aggie and Theo's.

From the other side of the door, where Bronwyn and

Adrian had escaped, long and slow screeching erupted from the metal, as though the creature was running fingernails—or claws—against it. Bronwyn stood still. Then a rapid scurrying sounded, followed by a cracking of wings. Even though she was in another room, she could almost feel the heavy wind against her face. The thing had entered their previous room, but Bronwyn had the key in her pocket. It hadn't beat down the doors, she and Adrian would have heard it. The creature must have come in through Aggie and Theo's room.

"It knows how to unlock doors?" Adrian whisper-shouted, eyes wide, jaw clenched.

"Right now, it's better for the demon-thing to be in that room instead of falling through our ceiling," Bronwyn whispered back and started searching around. Her heart beat so rapidly that she felt she may have a heart attack before escaping. Even if this had been a normal escape room attempt, her heart would've been on edge to win.

It was hard for her to think as she focused on the framed painted pictures decorating the rectangular room.

Adrian drew open a red toolbox and fished out a key. A silver box hung on the wall, and he put it in its lock. *Empty.*

"Fuck! Waste of time," he hissed.

Bronwyn started toward the wooden chair and the coffee table, where a fake king cake rested as the centerpiece, surrounded by colorful Mardi Gras coins. Just as she was about to reach it, the door behind her crashed open and her breath caught. But it wasn't from the room holding the creature.

Yan and Hollis stumbled through the door, fear on both their faces.

"What the hell is going on?" Hollis screamed, her curly hair disheveled.

Roars started and came to a crescendo, not from the one where the creature should have been, but from other places in the building, and it no longer sounded like just one. There had to be at least two.

"Quinn and Owen—" Yan started.

"Where are they?" Adrian interrupted, his tone bordering on frantic. The same as Bronwyn felt. She'd never seen him like this before. Hell, she'd never been like this before.

While waiting for a response, he continued searching around the room, doing what Bronwyn should have been doing too.

"Dead," Yan said, her lower lip wobbling. "Their bodies. These things. They killed them."

Bronwyn's heart palpitated so hard she felt as if it would burst, but she still leapt forward and slammed their door shut, not making the mistake of leaving it open. Her other two friends wouldn't be coming out now either...

"We'll figure it all out, but we're all together now, so we need to find a way to get the fuck out of here." Bronwyn hurried and plucked a picture of a jester off the wall. He sat on a throne, as if the world was his oyster. She shined the UV light on the back. No numbers.

The door across from them held another touchscreen lock, this time needing three numbers.

Bronwyn reached for the next painting covered in colorful masks and illuminated the light on it. Nothing. Yan had one in her hand, and Bronwyn brought up her light. *Nine.*

"Two more!" she shouted to Adrian who was searching with Hollis, both using their UVs.

The animalistic roars grew louder, closer. They had to be stirring from both rooms that each team had come out from. The growls became deafening, but she left her ears uncovered. Bronwyn wished that the people outside would hear them—they should hear them, but the place was soundproofed, and it was all supposed to be a game in good and fun. Yet, now it felt more than real, and that was because it was.

"Where is Simon?" Yan demanded.

Bronwyn just gave her a desperate look and shrugged while lifting the fake king cake and inspecting it. Either Simon was really dead, or he had managed to escape. Those were the only two conclusions that would explain why he hadn't opened the doors.

Adrian lifted a rug from the floor beneath the table and tossed it to the side, shining his light beneath it. Clenching his flashlight, he held up seven fingers.

Yan opened up a drawer on the other side of the table and fished out a small pocketbook. As she flipped through the pages, something rumbled as if it had catapulted into one of the doors. Licking her lips and thinking of anything but that, Bronwyn held up her UV light and watched as Yan turned and stopped.

"Four," Bronwyn whispered and shot to the padlock at the same time Yan did. They both started punching in numbers.

Seven. Nine. Four. *Denied.*

Seven. Four. Nine. *Denied.*

Nine. Seven. Four. *Denied.*

One of the doors burst open and Bronwyn glanced over her shoulder. The creature entered the room through the door Yan and Hollis had come from. They had to have left their box behind for the thing to get the code.

Charcoal gray body, wide face, animal and human all at once, broad wings that cracked like thunder as they flapped. With a strong body and dark veins, it looked like a demon gargoyle straight from Hell.

Nine. Four. Seven. *Denied.*

A high-pitched scream came from behind her. Hollis. She didn't look behind her, even though she wanted to, but she needed to get Adrian and Yan out to safety. Sweat beaded at Bronwyn's upper lip and temple.

Four. Nine. Seven.

Access granted. Unlocked.

A rough hand yanked Bronwyn back as Yan pushed open the door, her body flinging against the wall with a deafening smack. Her eyes dizzily made contact with Hollis's wide-open stare and slit-clawed throat. Adrian took a chair and struck it over the gargoyle's head, causing the beast to collapse to the side. With no hesitation, Adrian dropped the chair and yanked Bronwyn up from the floor. Yan waited for them at the entrance to the next room, gesturing them to hurry.

Bronwyn felt a hard shove from Adrian to her back, and she fell through the door. She scrambled to her feet and hurried to turn around to grab for Adrian. Just as she stood to reach for him, he was snatched back by the gargoyle like a little doll. True fear crossed his face as he looked at her, but not for himself, for her.

Yan pulled the door shut, and it locked automatically.

"No!" Bronwyn screamed, banging on the door as hard as she could to get it open. She could hear the shouts from Adrian, and then his silence, though the growling continued to fester.

Yan hauled Bronwyn back. "There's nothing we can do."

"You should have let me try and get to him!" Bronwyn cried, anger coursing through her veins.

"It was too late. I couldn't let you die, too." Yan sniffed, running a hand across her own cheek.

Bronwyn collapsed to her knees and let out a quiet sob at the same time Yan did. Both of the people they loved had just been murdered. She knew Yan loved Hollis as much as Bronwyn loved Adrian.

Five rooms total. There were five exit doors they had to get through, and they had already been through three. They were so close. Then what?

Taking a breath, Bronwyn didn't know if she could pick herself up to finish—all the while thinking about Adrian and how the cake she had baked him was downstairs sitting in the middle of the table. Now, he wouldn't ever get to eat that cake. She shouldn't have been caring about a fucking cake when he was dead—she wanted him with her. Somehow, she held back her emotions, chose to continue and cry later, *would* cry later, would probably *never* stop crying. Despite her thoughts screaming at her, she noticed the sounds from behind the door had stopped as well. For now, they were gone.

The room was dimly-lit, but brighter than the other ones had been. The door across required four numbers that they needed to hurry and find. There were boxes and boxes and more boxes scattered, all of the same color scheme—greens, purples, golds. A cot rested in the corner, with a thin striped mattress laying on top. Yan flipped through a stack of books in the corner of the room. Bronwyn hurried to lift the mattress and discovered words written in black marker.

Under the table.

She slapped the side of her leg. There wasn't a table

in the room!

Yan was still going through each book like her life depended on it—and it did. Bronwyn turned to the boxes and started removing the lids. In each box was one miniature item, the kind that belonged in a small dollhouse. Lamp. Rocking chair. Toilet. Bed. She tossed each toy and box to the side while Yan came and did the same. Dresser drawers. Dog. *Table*!

With quick motions, Bronwyn flipped the table over, hand trembling almost violently. Nothing. She shined the blue light on it and the code appeared. 5299.

"Got it!" she shouted and flew to the door. Her hand continued to shake as she pressed in each number. There were only four, but it felt like an eternity. *Access Granted.*

Bronwyn opened the door, and just as she let Yan pass, two large gargoyles smashed through the ceiling— wood and sheetrock raining down—and landed on their feet, wings flapping with devilish motions.

"Fuck!" Bronwyn yelled as she ran into the room and pulled the door shut—or thought she had. It wouldn't close. Her eyes grew wide as they settled on one of the gargoyle's hands. Sharpened talons protruded at the end of each finger. The creature let out a wild and furious shriek, tugging its hand back. She didn't hesitate and closed the door, the bolt sliding into place.

A look of horror crossed Yan's face. "They're coming through the ceilings now too?"

"One did that in Aggie and Theo's room," Bronwyn replied, her brow furrowed. The creatures had either went through the door or crashed through the ceilings. It was almost as if they were toying with them...

"This is the last room," Yan said, her chest heaving.

"Let's do this."

"Okay." Bronwyn frantically searched their surroundings. Streamers like the ones in the hallway hung from the ceiling, making the path hard to see with no visible light except for their flashlights. Bronwyn shined her regular flashlight and the UV one across the room. What covered the walls were rectangular mirrors with stickers displayed on them.

They couldn't stay here for long. Not when these things could unlock doors or crash through the ceilings, or do whatever it was they were doing. If this had been like any other year of their escape room attempts, Yan and Bronwyn would have battled to be the first one out the door. She wished Adrian was there with her in this last room like the year before.

Adrian. *Adrian.* Tears pricked at her eyes. She needed him. But he wasn't here. He was dead. Six of her other friends were dead—maybe seven, if Simon was. But Yan wasn't dead. And Bronwyn wasn't either. She needed to get them both out of here.

Beneath the floor came a heavy vibration—the gargoyles had to be striking their strong palms against the wood. The sounds of wings beating stirred all around the outside of the room, from above, from below, from the room where they had come, but not the exit. However, that didn't mean they weren't there or couldn't get there.

"I think I have a plan," Yan said. "Let's get the code and stay in here for a bit."

"Unless one gets in," Bronwyn finished. It was the smartest plan they had—they didn't know where in the building the gargoyles could be, or how quickly they could get there. But if there were more than two, which it sounded like there were, then they might pop out of anywhere.

"Focus on these stickers on the mirrors," Yan said, squeezing her locks of dark hair in desperation. "There has to be a reason they are on there. The shapes have to somehow become numbers by looking at them a certain way."

The stickers pressed to the glass were of a plastic baby, a crown, beads, each containing another sticker in the form of an arc above it. She peered at the sticker, not getting anything from it, but when she steered herself to the left, in the reflection, in the opposite mirror, a painted symbol formed a number.

"I see a three," Bronwyn rushed out the words, maneuvering herself to the crown next.

The beating on the walls, the ceiling, the floor, grew fiercer, louder.

"I got a seven!" Yan shouted.

Bronwyn's fingers tapped at her side, increasing in tempo. The arc across the top mixed with the image behind her created the number. "Two."

The exit to the final door didn't have a screen lock, but a place that needed a key. Bronwyn still had the one in her pocket from the first room, and she slid it in to see if it fit. It didn't.

Then what was the code for?

Bronwyn brushed streamers out of the way as she searched to the left. In the corner, there hung a box on the wall with a rotating number padlock on the front. She lifted it from its spot.

"Over here!" Bronwyn called, turning the numbers.

The beating increased, though she didn't know how that was possible because it was already so loud. Then the roaring started.

"Hurry!" Yan shouted.

"I'm trying!" Bronwyn clenched her teeth, rotating the numbers.

Seven. Three. Two. *No.*

Seven. Two. Three. *No.*

Something shot up from below them and Bronwyn shoved Yan to the side just in time as a shadow fell over her. The box fell from her hands and clanked to the floor.

The only thing she could think to do was kick the creature in the chest, and she did, making it shift back a fraction. A low growl reverberated through the room. She angled to the side and searched the floor as she ran, unable to find the box.

"I can't find it!" Bronwyn cried, her nerves more than on edge.

"Here!" Yan shouted, holding up a key.

A loud bang came from above as another gargoyle darted inside the room with a roar, followed by yet another. Three.

One grabbed Yan and made a clean slice with its claws across the olive skin of her throat. Bright red spilled out from the wound. Almost as if in slow motion, Bronwyn watched as the silver key fell from her friend's hand.

Bronwyn didn't even move for the key. She closed her eyes and waited to be next. All she heard was the sound of wings … and then nothing. The gargoyles had left, leaving Bronwyn alone. No, not alone, because when she opened her eyes, she found Yan's body.

She stared at Yan and rushed to her friend's side. There was no saving her—the gashes across her throat bled profusely and her eyes stared up, vacant. Bronwyn used her flashlight to find the key on the floor and sobbed as she plucked it up. She was alone. Earlier she had thought about winning, and now she had, but she no longer cared. All she wanted was to get out, but was it worth it with all her friends now murdered?

Maybe not. But she needed to try and warn people about the terrors going on if she could. She needed to warn the other Adrians, Yans, Hollises, Theos, Aggies, Quinns, Owens, and Simons of the world what was happening. These things could easily attack more people outside, if they hadn't already.

With heavy and exhausted limbs, she stood up and shuffled to the door. There, she inserted the key and turned it. Taking a deep breath, she twisted the knob, the sound seeming to be the loudest thing she'd heard all day, but that was all inside her head.

As she pulled open the door, Bronwyn breathed as quietly as she could. She peeked her head out into the hallway, looking left then right—empty. When she took a careful step forward, and then another, something dropped from the ceiling directly in front of her, with two horns, a sharp nose, and eyes of hazel. Eyes she knew so well. But it couldn't be. The wings beat behind him back and forth, causing her hair to stir.

"It looks like you won this year." He smiled, showcasing sharp teeth.

She recognized his voice, and then she knew for sure. A horrified gasp escaped her mouth, and she couldn't shift her gaze from those hazel eyes.

"How?" Her voice shook.

From behind her, noises multiplied, and she couldn't help but look over her shoulder, finding seven other gargoyles there. When she peered into the room that she was going to flee back into, Yan's body now lay broken into bloody pieces scattered around the room.

Bronwyn remembered the switchblade inside her pocket. She knew she might need it, but not for something like this. Keeping her attention on Adrian, she grabbed the weapon. She wrenched it out and pressed the button, the blade shooting out. Gritting her teeth, she shoved it directly into Adrian's strong chest, where it should have fractured his heart. It didn't even penetrate the skin, not even a scratch.

"Goodnight, my beautiful hellion." And Adrian's claws swiped across her throat.

Warm blood leached to the surface of her neck, and hot tears pricked her eyes. The world fell into purples and yellows and greens, matching the colors of the streamers hanging down the hallway. Then it all faded to black.

Bronwyn's eyes flicked open, and she felt cocooned, claustrophobic, trapped. She wiggled and roared until she lurched forward, ripping free from the shell she'd created and inhabited for that day, matching that of the human she'd eaten.

"Well, that was fun," she said, her wings beating against her back as she descended to the ground.

"I was so close this year…" Yan sighed from behind, her broad wings tight against her back.

"You always have next year," Bronwyn responded with a shrug, but inside she was beaming with joy.

When the lights flickered in the escape room, they all knew it was time to shut down their gargoyle side and tap into humanity by using the strength from what they had eaten earlier that day, forgetting what they truly were. It was a dangerous game, because if they had escaped without their humanity being killed, then they may not have ever discovered who they truly were. But it was a fun risk nonetheless.

Bronwyn remembered the terrified feelings she'd had when going through the rooms, and each year after they finished, she relished the rush. That feeling that she could die at any moment, but in the end, she didn't, because none of it was truly real. After they reawakened, they continued the game to terrify and catch whoever they could. It all began with Simon shifting first, who then picked the room to start in with the team who was the most behind. Which had to have been Aggie and Theo's because of their frolicking.

"How's your throat?" Adrian asked, his warm hand skimming across her thick skin, his talons brushing her neck.

"The same as yours was last year." She reached out and stroked the horns at his forehead, and grinned. "Now for the surprise I have for you downstairs."

"Oh yeah?" He cocked his head, his expression intrigued.

"Yes, my love. Follow me."

As the gargoyles descended the stairs, they discussed how the game could be improved the following year. Simon was already making a list—soundproof walls inside the rooms was at the top.

Once Bronwyn hit the last step, she walked to her place at the table and stood behind her silver dish, watching as the gargoyles moved behind theirs. Under each dish rested two organs that they had frozen from their victims. Usually, everyone had a heart and a kidney that they would eat when it struck midnight.

They didn't do this because they loved it, although they did. Each year on the start of Fat Tuesday or Mardi Gras, they had only a few days to feast, and they chose the humans because they could shift into that form for the year if need be.

"First," Bronwyn started, "I want Adrian to dig into the cake and find the gift I brought him."

"I know. I know." He chuckled. "They all have a baby Jesus inside."

"Just do it so we can eat already," Owen grumbled.

Shaking his head at Owen, Adrian drew the cake closer to him and placed his clawed hand inside. His talons circled, digging around, cake crumbs falling, until his hand stopped, finding what Bronwyn had been waiting for.

Clucking his tongue, Adrian lifted his hand and eyeballed the plastic baby nestled in his palm. She liked his expressions in the human form, but his gargoyle face was the one she truly loved. He was near perfect, beautiful, and dangerous. Like her, like their clan.

"It's a baby gargoyle." His lips tilted up at the edges. "Are you trying to tell me something?"

"Congratulations, my love." Bronwyn pressed her hands to her stomach. "You're going to be a daddy before next Mardi Gras."

Gasps escaped everyone around the room.

Mardi Gras was the annual night they had to feed, and next year they would be teaching their little one how to do the same.

"This is all amazing," Owen said, "but it's midnight already, so can we eat?"

Adrian smiled and pressed his lips to hers. "I told you in the letter that you would be getting a kiss at midnight."

He put his mouth to hers once more. "Or two."

"Now, let's eat." She grinned and slid on her Mardi Gras mask and watched as everyone did the same to celebrate the glorious occasion.

Thorna

*T*horna paced back and forth in the throne room while several of her beasties chopped pixies' bodies in half before draining their blood into buckets. Their sweet metallic odor filled the air. The pixies continued to eat the butterflies around Thorna's palace and if they would stay away, then they wouldn't have to die. But they were awful creatures.

She ignored their screams, the same as they did with the butterflies while murdering them. As Pyrka read over Thorna's next story, she contemplated rewriting a few of the ones she still hadn't given to Asher. But she decided against it, believing they were the stories that were meant to be told. Even if she made them seem more rosy, full of sunshine, it didn't seem like that would be a story from her. Life wasn't perfect, her kingdom wasn't either, so her tales would ring false if everyone was entirely jubilant. And she liked the darkness as much as she did the light.

"I want King Cake now," Pyrka said, licking his lips after reading her story.

She patted his head. "My favorite beastie, I shall bring you one soon." Her expression grew serious. "Can you do one more sweep to make sure the butterflies are still safe for the evening before going home?"

"Yes, my queen." He bowed and placed a palm over his heart.

This time when Thorna entered the mortal world, a chill lingered in the wind as she pumped her wings.

When she arrived at Asher's doorstep, she half expected another note to be there, yet there was nothing. After fishing out the scroll and thorns, she rang the doorbell but didn't dash away. A part of her itched to wait in her moth form. So she did just that, the heavy pads of Asher's feet echoing against the floor as he came to the door. He swung it open, his hair flopping everywhere, and peered down, seeming to already know another story would be there waiting for him.

Biting his lip, he scooped the scroll and twig up, then stared out into the night, scanning the area.

"Hey!" Asher called, his expression curious. "If you're there, just show yourself."

I am, Thorna said silently. It was true, even though she wasn't in a form where he would recognize her.

"Are you playing checkers by yourself?" Thorna asked, approaching the front desk in the antique store, a small Fabergé egg in her hand.

"Since I'm the only one here, yeah." Asher glanced up at her, amusement in his face as his lips tugged upward. "Unless ... you want to stay and play?" It came out more like a challenge, and she was always up for one of those.

Thorna had never once played any board game with a human, only her beasties. Even though she knew almost everything about the mortal world. "I suppose so," she said nonchalantly.

Asher motioned her around the counter and gave up his chair for her to sit while he grabbed another from the cluttered corner.

Taking a circular red checker piece, Thorna inched it forward. "Now make your move." He had to know she wasn't only referring to the game in that moment as her gaze remained locked on his alluring brown eyes.

A Little Wish

A hawk soared through the mist, its shrill cry reaching Jezka. She released her arrow. It shot straight through the eye of the beautiful hawk. *Strike one.* She watched as the bird tumbled to the dew-covered grass with a plop. Before heading back to her cabin to prepare supper, she would hunt two more.

After her parents passed away from the plague, she'd been completely alone, cooping herself up in her home away from everyone. Jezka had caught the plague too but recovered, although both physical and emotional scars were left in its wake. The ghost of the sickness still came to her at night when she dreamt of her lungs searching for air to breathe through her coughing, the painful boils on her body and her throbbing back. But then she would wake, chest heaving and cured.

Lifting her wool skirt, Jezka stepped over several red berry bushes. An ear-piercing screech reverberated from above. She crouched low, swiftly bringing up her bow, and released an arrow. Its sound quietly whistled in the air and pierced the hawk through the skull. *Strike two.*

She collected the bird from atop the fallen leaves and rested it on the dirt with her other kill.

The cool wind blew, tousling her long red curls. A village celebration was to be tonight, but Jezka wouldn't dare go. She used to venture to every one: eat, dance, then take a man back to the woods for a quick tumble.

But since her parents' deaths, Jezka had become more reclusive with each passing day. As though she were slowly becoming a ghost herself.

In a tree covered in pink blossoms, sitting high in its branches, another hawk preened its feathers. Jezka squinted her eyes, lifted the bow, then let her final arrow fly. It aimed true, sliding straight through the hawk's chest. *Strike three.*

The hawk tumbled downward, hitting a few limbs before landing on the ground with a sickening thump. She collected the bird, studying its elegant chestnut-colored feathers as she took it to the others.

After she removed the arrows from her kills, she placed them back in their quiver. Then using twine, she tied each of the hawks' legs together so she could easily carry them home.

As Jezka was about to place them over her shoulder, the light fog spilling through the woods grew thicker until she could scarcely see ten feet in front of her.

Through the ivory mist, a shadow stood in the distance. Jezka set the hawks down, then yanked an arrow out from its quiver and nocked it on her bow. The shadow drew closer, becoming a figure—a man. Dark hair spilled down his shoulders, his hazel gaze locked on her. The man's face was pleasant to look at with a strong jaw, chiseled cheeks, and a nose that may have been broken once before. A long pale-white scar ran down the left side of his face and over his eye, enhancing his features.

"What are you doing here?" the man asked, his voice deep.

"What am *I* doing here?" Jezka cocked her head. "You don't own these woods."

He smirked and arched a brow. "I certainly do."

"How so?" She narrowed her eyes, not lowering her bow as she stepped toward him.

"Follow me and see." He turned and walked back into the heavy fog, his outline becoming a shadow once more before he was gone.

Jezka snorted. She wasn't ignorant enough to follow a stranger into the woods. Turning on her booted heel, she left toward home, trekking through the fog with her supper.

As she walked, she thought about the man, his handsomely rugged face. If he'd been at the village dance before her parents had passed, she would have tumbled him after they were both drunk on ale. But she'd been a different person then—she didn't want to be careless and carefree anymore.

Once at home, Jezka plucked the feathers from the hawks and prepared them for the oven. As the birds cooked, she sharpened her arrow heads, the scent of roasted meat enveloping her.

When supper was ready, Jezka peeled off every sliver of meat from the hawks' bones until there was nothing left, and her belly was full.

As night fell, she stood, making her way through the silent house to her room. Lying on her bed, she gazed up at the ceiling, and thought once again about hanging herself from the beam. No one would find her. Not a single person would care she was gone. Her body would hang there until it was dust. Alone. Forgotten.

The next morning, Jezka headed for the woods, wondering if she would see the stranger again. She packed double the amount of arrows in her quiver in case she needed them, but she knew her aim was always true.

While passing a row of cottages, several with wet clothing hanging out to dry, her gaze settled on her best friend's home. After Jezka's parents had died, Sophia stopped coming to see her. In fact, Sophia hadn't tried to stay her friend much at all. Jezka's heart still hurt from it, almost as much as when her parents had died. But sometimes, one found out who a real friend was once an unforgettable event occurred.

A heavy fog blanketed the woods, just as thick as it had been the day before when she'd left. Jezka held tightly onto her bow while keeping her booted feet light. A few twigs snapped and leaves crunched beneath her feet. The fog would make it harder to find prey, but she rarely came home emptyhanded, even when it was like this.

As Jezka trekked farther into the woods, a rustling stirred. She held up her bow, a figure forming in the distance. The body drew nearer, and the stranger from the day before broke through the fog.

"Hello again." He smiled. "Did you come back to follow me this time?"

"I think I'll pierce your heart instead," Jezka said through gritted teeth. But a curious part of her did want to follow him, wanted to see where he would lead her. However, she wouldn't be foolish enough to do that.

The light fog darkened around her, growing heavier, changing from ivory to obsidian until she could see nothing. She spun around and around, not knowing where to point her arrow anymore. Her heart sped up and perspiration dotted her brow.

Then her eyes became heavy, drifting shut. Jezka's body fell to the side on the ground, her bow slipping from her hands. Two strong arms scooped her up, and she didn't have the strength to scream as she felt herself being lowered into something. But the man didn't release his hold on her.

Jezka peeled open her eyes and focused on a bright light. She lifted her heavy head, finding the man carrying her down a stone staircase in one arm while his other was outstretched, holding a lantern in his hand.

After what felt like hours, the stranger set Jezka back on her feet. Her body swayed before her strength returned. Lanterns around her flickered to life, their flames bobbing. She didn't have the urge to run, not when her curiosity grew at what she was seeing. Shelf after shelf was lined with dolls. Hundreds of them. Their shining metal faces reflecting the lanterns' light, their silvery eyes seeming to follow her, their frozen smiles like grimaces, silent pleas for her to help mend them.

Some were missing limbs, hair, their toothless mouths gaping wide—while others appeared pristine, as though ready to be given to a child, a special gift on their birthday.

Jezka took a deep swallow, placing a hand at her pounding heart. "Are you some kind of doll maker?"

"You could say that." He folded his arms and stepped toward her.

"What is this place?"

"A long-forgotten tower that was built beneath the earth. It will grant anyone a little wish."

Sophia had always believed these woods were haunted, and she'd never once come with Jezka. Perhaps she'd been right.

"Do you haunt these woods?" Jezka asked, a strange feeling taking root in her chest. Although, not fear. "Are you some kind of ghost?"

"You could say that," he repeated his earlier words. "But it's only to give wishes. I come to those in need of a wish, and by the empty and lost look in your eyes, I'm offering you one, if you want it."

Her stomach sank as she thought about her parents, and what she'd become this past year. No longer herself, the carefree girl she remembered. Perhaps it was mostly her fault Sophia didn't want to come visit Jezka anymore. But if the roles had been reversed, Jezka never would have stopped trying to help her friend.

Jezka blinked several times, locking her gaze on the stranger's hazel eyes. "What's your name?"

"Zel." His lips tugged up on one side. "And you?"

"I'm Jezka."

"Beautiful name." He paused, biting his lower lip. "Do you want to use your wish?"

A wish... Would it work? Jezka had experienced something supernatural above, when the fog changed from white to black. Then there was this man before her, who was possibly a ghost or something else... Yet, what did she have to lose? She had no one anymore. "It can be anything?"

Zel nodded. "Anything at all."

Jezka thought about something she would want to wish for. She didn't know if what this man spoke was the truth. If she could have her parents back, she would. But she wasn't going to wish to have anyone return from the dead. There wasn't anything else she truly wanted, not when she'd just ached for death the night before.

He held out his palm and Jezka didn't hesitate as she placed hers in his, feeling his coldness. She shivered at the touch, but didn't want to release her grasp.

"A kiss first?" Zel whispered, studying her beneath thick lashes.

A kiss? Jezka studied his shapely lips, ones that she knew without kissing would expertly mold and move against hers. "Is that required?"

"No. I only want to taste you."

Jezka had tumbled several strangers in her past, and she wanted to kiss him too. Perhaps to see what a ghost, or whatever he was, tasted like. It had been too long since she had touched anyone. She licked her lips and nodded.

Zel then leaned forward and brushed his lips softly against hers. It didn't stay chaste for long as she explored his mouth with her tongue. Her hands cradling his face, gripping his hair. His fingers trailing up and down her spine. And then she pulled back, even though her body yearned for more.

"I wish not to be lonely anymore," Jezka murmured.

Zel closed his eyes as though something pained him. "You should have refused the wish."

Before she could speak, a tickling sensation crawled beneath her skin, through her entire body. She peered down to find a shiny silver color spreading across her flesh before hardening. Not only that, but everything around her became larger as she shrunk smaller and smaller until she was the same height as Zel's boot.

With a heavy sigh, Zel scooped her from the floor. He placed her on the shelf in between two other metal dolls, then tenderly stroked her cheek. Something like regret shone in his eyes. "I am free now. But you will be trapped here, released only to roam the woods in search of your replacement. I pray someday, perhaps, we can meet again, when that day of freedom comes. I'm ... I'm sorry."

Zel's shoulders hunched as he walked away, slowly ascending the stairs. Jezka screamed inside her head, begging for him to come back.

Yet she was no longer alone in a room full of dolls.

Thorna

"What happens next?" Pyrka asked, placing the story on the table beside her throne. "Does Jezka ever get to leave the woods?"

"Ah." Thorna chuckled. "I always know what will happen next but as for you and Asher, it will be wherever your imagination leads you." She would never give up what comes after the ending to anyone. Not even Asher.

"If he doesn't choose you, then he's a fool," Pyrka said, straightening and puffing out his chest.

"We can all be fools." She patted his head and sank down into her throne. "Go home and rest. Have a good night with your family."

After Pyrka left, Thorna remained in the throne room, watching the butterflies circle one another, dancing and loving. They looked like darkness—they looked like pure loveliness. They were her lovely grim.

Thorna finally shifted and flew through the water wall. Tonight, for some reason, the mortal world smelled of shattered hearts and darkened dreams. There were so many beautiful things, but so much ugliness too. More so than her world.

Even though she wanted to wait for the door to open or to peer into Asher's window, she left him his gifts and barreled back home. Thorna started doubting herself, wondering if she should have given the stories all at once. But she wanted to do it this way, not simply lure him to her kingdom. She wanted to do something with meaning. For him.

"What do you do?" Asher asked, clearing his throat. "Like are you in college or do you work?"

"I'm in charge where I am." Thorna shrugged and pushed a checker piece forward. Every day, they would play a game. Sometimes cards, others Chinese checkers or chess. It was a slow and melodic way of getting to know one another. The perfect way. When customers came in, she no longer left, but would help him around the store.

"So secretive." He chuckled, brushing a lock of hair from his face.

"One has to be at times."

"If you refuse to let me pay you for helping me, then take something you want each day."

"I can't deny that offer." She eyed the new box of teacups he had gotten in, wondering which one she would choose.

He noticed her looking at the cardboard box. "I would give them all to you today, but then you might not come back."

"That might be true." Thorna winked. However, she would keep returning, yet not only for the teacups.

A Layer Hidden

"And in the end the princess kissed the prince awake," Bree whispered, watching her pride and joy breathe in and out, her delicate chest lifting and falling. She kissed her daughter's warm forehead before slowly backing away, careful to not wake her.

"Mommy?" Kattie asked, her soft brown eyes opening sluggishly. They looked as though they would collapse back down at any moment.

"I'm right here, in the bed next door." Bree smiled. "Remember, we're roommates for a little while longer."

"I had a dream." Kattie adjusted her shoulders, her tangled chestnut-colored locks fanning in all directions.

"What kind of dream?" Bree leaned forward, curious. Kattie always had the most vivid and colorful imagination.

"My eyeball fell out." She blinked as though checking to see if they were both still there. They were.

"That sounds more like a nightmare to me." Bree had nightmares of her teeth pouring out from her mouth, but never once losing an eyeball. Even in sleep, she had the most creative child.

"But I wasn't scared," Kattie hurried on. "I just dealt with having one eye as if it had always been that way."

"That's good." Bree pressed her fingers to Kattie's lids and drew them shut. "Both your eyeballs are still intact. Now get some rest."

"What do you think the new world will be like?"

"Hopefully better than the last. But humans have a tendency to destroy things, and you should know that, just so you're prepared in case this planet becomes awful, too."

"We'll help to take care of this one better. I love you, Mommy."

"I love you, Kattie Kat."

Bree padded to her bed and sat on the edge. She glanced over her shoulder, where she found her husband, Will, already fast asleep. As she slid beneath the covers, finding herself comfy and shutting her eyes, a shuffling sounded from outside the door. She ignored it, but then a buzzing came, drifting up like a swarm of bees. She shot out of bed and yanked open the door. Nothing. Not a bee. Not a person. Only an empty hallway.

She searched left and then right while gripping the handle, the pale-yellow glow of the night lights guiding her sight. Above her, one of the orbs flickered, and Bree chalked it up to that being the sound she'd heard. "We pay all this money for the voyage and they can't even have decent lights that work," she grumbled.

Quietly, she shut the door and tiptoed back to bed, careful not to disturb Will or Kattie.

In between the dream state and the real world, Bree's body seemed to float until she felt something lightly slither its way up her thigh, causing her eyes to flick open and tug her back into reality.

Bree's stiff shoulders relaxed when she realized it was just Will's hand trailing up her leg, trying to get some action *again*. His firm length pressed against her hip, and she rolled her eyes as she casually moved his arm back to his side. But then his hand crept toward her once more. Bree smiled and turned over before nudging Will in his ribs.

He stirred for a moment, grunted, then went back to sleep. So this time, she pulled her elbow up and jabbed him harder in the arm when he poked against her again. Will's eyes flew open in the almost-darkened room, highlighted by a night-light on the wall across from the bed. Bree couldn't do without one, even though she was a grown woman.

"What the hell was that for?" Will asked, his voice rough from sleep. He brought the heel of his hands to his eyes and rubbed them.

"Shh, you don't want to wake Kattie." Bree suppressed her laugh. "You were doing it again." It was the fourth night in a row where she'd awoken to him wanting to score. She understood—she would have liked to as well. Weeks on a ship headed for their new home planet with their ten-year-old daughter in the same room was no canister of sunshine. However, Bree was old enough to control her hormones for the remainder of the journey. Will, on the other hand, still had the sex drive of when they'd first met.

"Sorry, I can't help it." He was already trying to drift back to sleep as he turned to his stomach, eyelids fluttering.

"Just a few more days, and I promise for the first week I'll make it up to you when Kattie's in her own room," Bree said with a widening smile. That caused Will's eyes to open a little more. She hadn't thought it would be that bad to share a room with their daughter. It wouldn't have been either, but the room was tiny even for one person, and the days had been long aboard the ship after they'd left Earth. Bree had even found herself space sick a few times, expelling the contents of her stomach on several occasions.

"I'll hold you up to that promise." Will chuckled softly while gently rubbing Bree's thigh.

Bree sat up and slowly dragged her fingertips across Will's face and pressed her body against his, teasing them both. "Since I'm already awake, I'm going to get something to eat and drink in the lounge. Do you want anything?"

"My throat is a little parched. I'll take some water." Tilting his chin toward the ceiling, he rubbed at his neck like he'd never had a sip of liquid in his entire life.

"Aww, my poor baby is thirsty. I'll bring you back a little drink," she said in a sarcastic motherly voice and grinned while patting his arm.

"Just the way I like it," he whispered seductively, his hand at her lower back, his fingers dipping into the waistband of her pajama pants.

"Enough with the *Psycho* foreplay already before you try to get frisky again." Leaning over, she held her smile and gave him a gentle peck on the lips. As she pulled away, he tugged her down for one more sweet kiss, his warm lips tasting hers as if they were his water. She returned the embrace eagerly, running her hand over his shorn hair. She still missed his long locks, but she also liked that she could see his cheek bones and jawline better now.

Bree loved Will now as much as she had thirteen years ago when she'd met him at eighteen. They'd gotten married at twenty, and everyone told them they were too young. Well, who was laughing now? They were still together and just as happy as they'd been back then. Her heart still beat for his, the way his did for hers, even though life had gotten more complicated. *But that's what happens as you grow up*. Kattie was lucky to still get to be a child for a while longer.

Pushing back the thin blankets, Bree kicked them off her and stepped out of the bed. Before she left, she walked across to where Kattie lay sleeping. She stood there for a moment, listening for her daughter's soft breathing until she heard it. With a small sigh, she tiptoed the remainder of the way toward Kattie, and reached over to stroke her hair, finding it a little damp. Bree wondered what Kattie was dreaming about to cause the beads of perspiration on her forehead. Was it the missing eyeball nightmare returning or something else? She lowered her hand and felt Kattie's forehead to make sure there was no fever. The skin was cool to the touch, and Bree let out another relieved breath.

Kattie had suffered from seizures since she was six months old. They used to occur every month until they, thankfully, became sparser. It had been three years since her last one, but Bree still panicked every time Kattie developed a fever, since it was a precursor to the seizures. That was why she still found herself checking on Kattie every so often, just to make sure she wasn't sick. Even though her daughter was ten, when Bree looked down at her, she still saw the baby girl she'd first held in her arms. And that feeling would never go away.

Bree leaned down to give Kattie a light kiss on the forehead, vowing to bring her back a cold water to sit by her bedside in case she needed it.

First thing first though was the bathroom—she had to

pee like a racehorse and had no time for leakage, so she hauled butt to relieve herself. Finding herself a little more relaxed after doing her everyday business, she silently left the room, and glanced at her loved ones one more time before she shut the door behind her with a soft click.

In only a few days' time, they'd be arriving on the new planet, Sorsa. Earth had become more overcrowded over the last several decades, and when Sorsa was discovered and visited, things looked up for mankind. Bree didn't think her family would be one of the lucky people chosen, but they had been after she'd entered the raffle. She and Will were given new jobs and Kattie would be attending the private school that was built there. Everything was falling into place.

The gorgeous pictures and unpolluted lands were the main reasons Bree had applied. Fresh air and no longer having to wear oxygen masks when going outdoors. The Sorsa crew had only been accepting families with at least one child at the time, so they were a perfect match.

Outside the room, the poorly-lit hall had become darker. The flickering must have spread and somehow knocked the entire row out. As Bree pressed her hand to the smooth wall, she stumbled over something on the floor and kicked it to the side, not being able to see what it was. But it felt soft.

While walking through the dark, it seemed as if an eternity had gone by. *Can't someone come out and fix this?* she thought to herself as her movements sped up. Luckily, just up ahead, a glowing light came into view.

Rounding the sharp corner, Bree released hold of the wall when she entered the large lounge. The open area was decorated in neat rows of silver circular tables, each surrounded by four metal chairs. Other than the tables, everything else was alabaster with a single white clock on all four walls, as though someone could easily lose track of the time.

None of the clocks were digital either—they were all old-school with long metal hands that repeatedly *tick-tick-ticked*. She'd held a pocket watch once but never had an actual mechanical clock in her household. However, she loved old antiques and old horror films from decades and decades past.

She scanned the area and expected to see a few of the usual familiar faces, but no one was around. The previous nights when Bree would venture out of her room after being woken by Will's advances, there were always at least a couple other people in here, or at least someone working behind the counter.

Bree marched up to the counter, her bare feet feeling sticky against the ceramic floor. Across the white countertop, an unknown green substance lingered that resembled jelly. She ignored the questionable substance and peered over the edge, hoping she wouldn't catch a fright if the worker popped out. But no one was there. Shrugging to herself, she leaned back and figured maybe they were off getting some action, or maybe some sleep of their own. The one thing she didn't like aboard the ship was that technology was nonexistent. No screens, no phones. Everything had to be stored in the belly beneath the ship.

The familiar buzzing crackled from the lights above and as she peered up, two hands grabbed her by the waist. She let out a scream and whirled around, prepared to punch the person in the face. Only to find Will chuckling at her.

"Boo," he said.

"Boo my ass. What are you doing?" She scanned the area, waiting for people to come out of their rooms to ask why she'd been screaming. But everyone must've been too deep in sleep or didn't care to see if she'd just been murdered.

"You were taking too long with the water."

"I literally just stepped into the lounge, you impatient man."

"No, Kattie Kat woke up, drenched in sweat and saying she needed water. So here I am, hero and bringer of water."

Bree's hand flew to her chest, her heart slamming against her palm. "Is she sick?"

"No fever, just thirsty, Bree. Like me, like you. Don't worry so much." He gave her a soft peck on the nose.

Will took three bottled waters from the refrigerator and handed her one. "Looks like no one's around if you want me to come back after dropping off the water." He waggled his eyebrows.

She cocked her head. "Really?"

"You know I'm just kidding." He walked backward with a smile. "Or am I?"

"Do you want me to check on her with you, though?"

"No, you sit out here, eat, relax, and I promise I'll stay awake and look after her until you come back. Then you can kiss me goodnight again before we both drift off, preferably a long one like the princess gave to the prince in the story." His grin grew wider, daring.

"So you were awake during the story?"

"Hey, it was an interesting one."

Bree rolled her eyes. "The kiss was a peck."

"We can make it our own version then." He blew her a kiss and chuckled before leaving.

"When you get back," she called, "can you buzz the crew and tell them the lights are off in the hall and this one out here started flickering?"

"Will do."

Blowing out a breath, Bree pushed away from the counter and walked over to the clean white cabinets. She opened the first one, a squeak echoing throughout the area. Inside, she sifted through, finding all sorts of healthy snacks. There were no goods, so she immediately closed that one, not in the mood for those nasty types of treats. With a pivot, she scooted to the next one, discovering it to be stacked with coffee supplies. *Gross.* While sticking out her tongue like a child, she closed that one even faster.

Quickly, she pulled open the third cabinet, wishing for anything fattening and amazing. *And*, she'd hit the jackpot. Bree snatched a couple snack cakes with fierce precision as though they'd disappear before she made contact. She closed the door, apologizing in advance to the next lone person who would enter it since she took the last of the sweets.

Bree opened her bottle of water and swigged half of it down as she shuffled her way to one of the small tables. Pulling back a chair, she sank down and propped her feet up on the metal of another seat while crossing her ankles.

Dark locks of hair swung forward and she brushed them aside while unwrapping her delicious treat. The plastic crinkled and the sweet smell radiating off the frosting hit her nose.

Before the softness touched her tongue, the light above flickered, startling Bree for a moment. Glancing around the room like she'd discover the bandit who committed the crime, she found nothing.

Oh, well. She shrugged to herself, hoping Will had gotten ahold of someone to fix the light problem. If she had to call down to them, she wouldn't be as nice as Will. She wasn't an angry person in general, but with that sort of thing she could be.

Finally, she got the bite she so desperately wanted. Mid-chew, the light flickered again. Bree whipped her head up toward the ceiling, when a buzz came again, and this time wouldn't stop. Annoyance hit her then, maybe even a bit of anxiety kicked in, too. What if the ship lost all its power? What if the ship never made it to its destination? What if the ship blew up? The thought of being trapped in space haunted her to the core.

Silence surrounded her again, and she wished someone else was in the lounge. Maybe she should have asked Will to stay, or to bring Kattie with him. No, they both needed their rest.

Hurriedly, she stuffed the remainder of the cake into her mouth and chewed fast, taking a larger swallow than she should have. Coughing, Bree reached for the bottled water. She hastily opened it and took a heavy swig to help push the cake down. It worked. *Dying from choking would have been a shitty way to go.*

She gasped and stood from the chair, the buzzing still ringing in her ears. Just as she took her first step, the last of the lights disappeared. Enveloped in darkness, she remained as still as a statue, but then realized that was ridiculous. It was only a little dark, nothing to fear. She was a grown woman, yet one who still needed a night-light after the sun set. She remembered her mother locking her in a dark closet when she was younger, saying she needed to be disciplined. Bree had chosen to be nothing like her mother when she'd become pregnant with Kattie.

In the dark, something rustled, causing her to continue standing frozen. The noise came again, a scurrying and pitter-patter across the floor. It had to be her imagination. When she used to be in that closet, she'd always imagined things, but they'd never sounded this real, this near.

Her heartbeat kicked the inside of her ribcage, and she took a couple steps in the dark. Bree's muscles, her blood, her veins all felt the increased pump when her heart beat again. Another patter came, growing in sound as whatever it was drew closer. Bree held her breath, careful to not make any noise.

Right when she was about to take off running, to get away from whatever was lurking around, most likely a stowaway rat, the lights flashed back on, blinding her. From her peripheral, she could see something shifting on the floor. She spun to the side, her eyes clearing and focusing on a baby girl on all fours crawling, smiling at her.

Tight red curls surrounded the head and bright green eyes gazed into hers. Bree smiled back at the baby. But then her smile dropped as she searched around the room for the mother or father. *The baby must've somehow snuck out of her room and crawled in here.*

"Where did you come from?" Bree asked, hurrying to the child. If Kattie had crawled off somewhere when she was a baby and Bree discovered her missing, she would have had a panic attack. She needed to find the baby's parents before they became too scared.

As she inched closer to the child, something seemed off when she scanned the face more closely. Thin lines, resembling cracks, etched the baby's face, arms, and legs, as though someone had drawn on her. *That can't be right.* But it was right.

Heart accelerating, Bree bent down and scooped the baby girl off the cold floor, never taking her eyes away from the child's green irises. Bree's breaths increased as she observed the child's skin. She could now clearly see the fissures all over her, not drawn on lines with a writing tool. She had to find someone. *Now.*

Lifting a hand to touch the baby's warm cheek, to let her know things would be okay, Bree brushed across the warm delicate skin. Under her fingertips, she could feel the separation of skin and was pretty sure that things were *not* okay.

Just as Bree pulled her hand back from the cheek, the baby snapped forward with a hiss and an open mouth, almost too wide. It took only a split-second to draw herself out from the stunned moment, but when she did, Bree *screamed.* Bright red dripped down the child's lips and chin as she lunged again. Bree dropped the baby, then dragged her hand to her face, shaking, seeing blood—the red on the baby's lips was from Bree.

Fingers.

Her fucking three fingers were gone, all the way to the base. Thick blood oozed out from the wounds, and she stared in horror at her pinky and thumb that were still there. Her eyes fluttered as panic sewed its way throughout her entire body, in her bones, her nerves, her muscles, her skin. Then she peered down at the baby on the floor who wasn't coming after her, but instead convulsing on her side. Bree's fingers were nowhere in sight, the thing must've swallowed them.

It was as if Bree was frozen in terror, unable to remove her eyes from the child on the floor. *Something's not right*, she thought as her hand throbbed and shook frantically.

The baby's trembling calmed. From the child's face, a chunk of skin peeled away and fell to the floor, revealing green muscle beneath. Was the baby *molting*? Another few pieces slid off and spiraled downward.

The baby continued to hatch out of its skin, then rolled and crawled toward her, leaving a trail of green slime in her wake that matched the mysterious spot on the counter Bree had seen earlier.

Why am I still standing here?

The shock wore off, and Bree needed to get help as her hand continued to throb. She took off toward the front of the ship to warn the crew that they needed to do something. Arrest the baby? She didn't know! It was too insane to think about.

As she tore down the hall, she cradled her hurt hand to her chest, all the while shouting for someone, anyone. Not a single door opened. Why were they ignoring her? Had they encountered the baby?

"Hello!" she yelled as her legs pumped and her bare feet hit the cool ceramic floor. But then she stopped in her tracks when her gaze met pools of blood seeping out from the bottom of several doors.

Chest heaving, Bree tried to unlock both doors to see if anyone needed help, but they were locked. She avoided the blood and continued down the hall to the crew's working quarters at the front of the ship.

The door was already slid open. She paused. It should've been closed, and she should have to hit the button to retrieve a crew member.

Bree felt the need to run back to her room now, but she had to warn the crew of the strangeness, because if not, things could potentially get worse. *But it's only one mutated baby. And whatever else caused blood to leak out under doors!*

As she slipped inside the area, empty white tables with red handprints slid into view. Her gaze dropped to the floor, where bodies were sprawled about. Three women and two men wearing white uniforms splashed with red. All of them stared wide-eyed in slumped positions with holes in their chests and body parts ripped off.

Bree swung her unhurt hand to cover her mouth, bile rising up her throat. This couldn't be happening. She hurried past the dead bodies, sharp stings radiating through her hand. Up front, in the cockpit, she found the three pilot chairs, each holding a body tilted over, soaked in blood.

A choking breath echoed. Bree gasped and darted toward the hurt woman.

"What do you need?" Bree asked, making sure to not touch her. "What happened?"

"The—the—chi—"

Bree didn't get to hear the rest because the woman's breaths stopped. There was no one, no one at all, piloting the ship. Only the dead.

Will. Kattie. She had to get to them.

When she rushed back out of the room, past the strewn bodies, to the hallway, the lights were flickering. All the doors opened. The lights shut off completely before Bree could have a peek inside. A stirring came from each room.

She didn't stand around to wait for what happened, she took off on a hard sprint down the darkened hall, praying to make it back to her room safely. Not for her life, but to warn her loved ones.

When she turned the corner, the lounge was still lit, the trail of the green gore on the floor leading to the counter. A growl and gurgle sounded there, and she didn't stop to see what the monster baby was doing.

As Bree was about to turn the corner to take the hall back to her room, several little people coming to her shoulder stepped into view, blocking her path. When she inched closer, they were possibly children, causing her to gasp. Bree's gaze bounced around, searching for the molting baby who could sneak up on her, but she came up empty. Her attention focused on the sickly green children who stood in front of her, staring, hissing. Or maybe they weren't children, but some monstrous form who looked as though all their skin had been wiped away, leaving only muscle showing. The hue was of a deep green, the color of the darkest leaves on a tree that could be found on Earth.

Behind her, the stirring did come then, the snapping baby had made a comeback. Three green monster children, one vicious baby, her missing fingers. *I can do this.* Bree took off on a mad dash, barreling toward the three creatures—she was going to knock them down like bowling pins.

When Bree collided, instead of the children breaking apart, she was thrown back by their strength. Her body flew several feet away, landing smack on her tailbone. A sharp pain raced up her spine, and a small squeak escaped her lips.

She turned to the side, her eyes meeting the mutated baby crawling toward her, completely green and bald, growling and hissing. Not wanting to lose what was left of her fingers, Bree pushed up to her feet, stumbling her way back to the little monsters standing in the hall.

"What's going on here?" she asked the three children while avoiding Snapping Baby.

One of the creatures took a step forward, leaving Bree almost enough of a space to break through. She couldn't tell if the green child was a boy or girl because there was no hair on the head, and the features seemed to blend in with its coloring. The child wore a cotton white shirt with matching pants, as did the other two who stood beside him or her.

"We are taking over. It's time for you to say goodnight," the monster child spoke matter of fact, the sides of its lips pulled downward.

"Well, yes, goodnight sounds fantastic. Let me head to my room now." Bree lunged one more time, but the child was prepared. Latching on to Bree's wrist with the missing fingers, the child squeezed to the point where she couldn't feel the throb of the missing fingers any longer.

"This is what we needed. Bodies. But yours won't do for us." The green child's eyes also glowed emerald, like that of the baby. In fact, they all did.

Before Bree could say anything, a loud crack echoed in the room. It happened too fast—Bree couldn't breathe. The piece of shit had snapped off her hand just above her wrist like a tree branch. The howl of agony then came. She needed to vomit—her precious cake from earlier rose up her throat and spewed on the child's bare green feet.

Repulsed, the monster child backed away, and Bree took the opportunity to dart past what she could only assume were a green murderous cult. Her wrist pulsed where the hand was missing, and her skin grew paler by the second while blood leaked out.

"Your time is coming," the child seethed down the hall.

"No, your time will be coming once I get my hand wrapped up and find a gun, you little shit," she murmured to herself as she hurried down the darkened hallway.

Breathing heavily, she strained to find her door. As soon as her hand reached the handle at the end of the hallway, she pushed it open. Lungs hurting, everything hurting, she rushed inside and slammed the door behind her, locking it. She needed to wake Will and Kattie immediately.

Her entire body shook as she pressed the button for light. A bright beam spread through the room, and Bree trembled as her eyes tried to adjust, her brain unsteady from all that had occurred.

She blinked as she studied the floor. Her blinks became rapid as she saw what looked to be tan skin. Her eyebrows drew together while her body swayed, making her feel as though she was a Hawaiian dancer, or a drunken one, from the blood loss.

Bree's brain wouldn't connect the pieces of what the skin on the floor meant. And then it did. Her head snapped up toward where Will lay on the bed. She backed into the door, her handless arm flying to her mouth as a half-cry, half-scream gurgled out.

Green. A green child stood hovering over a bloodied Will. Her husband's chest was a torn mess, bone exposed, a still heart resting next to the body.

"Kattie," Bree whispered. She had to get her and prayed to all things supernatural that her daughter was all right and not torn to pieces. Her eyes angled to Kattie's bed, finding it empty with a huge wet spot and blankets crumpled on the floor.

Bree's hand continued to tingle with numbing pain as her gaze went from the bed, to the skin on the floor, to the green child who was now watching her with intensity.

Hands drenched in Will's blood, dripping, dripping, the green child stepped toward her, wearing a white nightgown that matched Kattie's. "Hello, Mother."

"Shit." Bree began to sob—she didn't understand what was happening. Somehow this green monster was Kattie, and her normally brown eyes were now the same emerald shade as the other children from the lounge.

Kattie took several slower steps toward Bree while shaking her hand to the side. Something happened, and Kattie's bloodied fingers now resembled sharpened daggers coming to a deadly point.

"Sorry, Mother. We need these bodies for our home planet. Yours is past puberty, so it's unusable."

Home planet? They were aliens... "I don't understand. Where's Kattie?" Bree looked one more time at her handsome husband who would never speak his beautiful and hilarious words to her again, then back at this monster that had taken her sweet daughter.

"Kattie's gone." Using one swift thrust, the creature shoved her knife-like fingers into Bree's chest. With a now mostly empty rib cage, Bree sank to the floor as all her good memories turned into emptiness.

Thorna

"That was a dark treat." Pyrka folded the story in half and placed it on her table.

"Why thank you, Pyrka." Thorna knelt in front of him. "We may have vicious things here but, thankfully, not strange alien children to take over our bodies.

He shuddered and made a rumbling noise in his throat.

Thorna laughed. The butterflies swirled around her, their movements growing frenzied, hungry. "For now, the pixies seem to have learned their lesson, so the butterflies will have to drink the blood from the thorns. Can you gather the other beasties to help you squeeze the crimson out?"

"Of course, my queen." Pyrka bowed and lifted one of the empty buckets from the dirt ground. The blood in the thorns wasn't as sweet as a pixie's, but it was delicious all the same.

"I'll return in a little while," Thorna said before transforming and breaking through the water barrier. She wouldn't go home straight away this time—she would circle the forest for a bit after leaving Asher's. To think. She hadn't been to the antique store in days and she missed seeing him, talking to him. Did he wonder when she would come back?

Thorna thought about the story she was going to give him tonight—this tale was close to her heart, one that she could relate to in a way. Even now she wondered if what she was doing was foolish. Perhaps she should leave the mortal alone, let him be. But fae were selfish creatures too, just as humans could be.

As she dipped down toward Asher's home, a familiar scent washed over Thorna, her heart a ravenous organ as it pounded away inside her. On the porch with his back against the door, his feet flat on the ground, his legs open, sat Asher. One hand gripped his hair while the other studied his phone. He looked positively perfect, and in that moment, she wanted to shift to her fae form, remove her clothing, let him peel down his, feel their bodies, flesh to flesh, warm against one another. But she didn't know what to do now since she was still in her moth form. Should she wait, go home, or show herself?

Flapping her wings, Thorna lowered herself onto a green fern in the garden, still able to see Asher. She lingered there and waited for him to go inside, but he remained where he was. Eventually his eyes closed, his breathing growing even.

Thorna swooped up from the bush and drew closer to Asher, so close that her moth legs almost brushed his face. She wanted to—she wanted to feel every inch of him.

Instead, she shifted, peering down at him. Her heart quickened as she rested the new scroll and twig beside him. Thorna then traced his lips with her fingertip, and his breathing hitched, even in sleep. Smiling, she tapped his cheek, then transformed back into the moth just before Asher cracked open his eyes.

"Do you have a girlfriend?" Thorna asked, curious. Asher had never mentioned a female, but that didn't mean he didn't have someone.

"No." He smiled. "My last girlfriend was about six months ago. We separated on good terms though. What about you? Are you seeing anyone?"

"No." Thorna thought about her last lover. She had killed him when he tried to take over her kingdom—she wouldn't get into that just yet, though. But one day. However, all her lovers weren't fools. Most she had also parted with on good terms—they just weren't meant to last.

"So we're both single then..." Asher's smile grew wider.

Nothing but Bones

Bones crunched beneath Irin's fatal touch. Screams echoed across the swells of the lake.

Irin pierced the man's throat with her sharp fangs, then drank every drop of his blood. His movements stilled. She lifted a hand and using her sharp nails, tore into his flesh, peeling it apart piece by piece before shoving each layer into her mouth. Until only his skeleton peered back at her. To the outside world, the man would become just another who had vanished from his boat.

Suicide, they would claim. Drowning, they would cry.

Although for this one, his body would never be found.

Irin had been alone in these waters since the beginning of time. She could take the form of any sea creature she wished. Only once had she made the mistake of being caught when she'd chosen to grow in size to a great sea beast with a long curving neck and smooth silver flesh.

Lochness Monster, they had shouted. Kill it, they had demanded.

But she made sure the monster was never seen again.

Since that day, Irin had stayed to shifting into creatures beneath the water that weren't as noticeable to villagers.

Swallowing her last bite of bloody meat, Irin pulled

the dead man's skeleton down to the bottom of the lake. She kicked her scaled legs but it wasn't fast enough, so she sprouted a tail that would make the villagers above scream mermaid if they spotted her.

Irin's pace picked up as she flicked her tail, swimming past colorful fish and striped eels. Her dark hair remained swept back, skimming her waist.

Once she reached the gritty texture of the lake floor, she broke apart the skeleton into smaller portions and buried them.

Irin's hair floated around her as she swiped her forehead and studied a small shark circling an eel before swimming north. If she hadn't recently eaten, it would have made a fine meal to tear into. Her eyelids fluttered and she angled her gaze to the hidden cave that had been her home for as long as she could remember. Flicking her tail, she swam to her cave and entered the dark space. She allowed her eyes to focus so she could see into the blackness. Nothing ever crept inside there—not even a single fish, as if they knew the danger they would face.

Settling her body into the sandy bottom, Irin stared at the bare walls around her. Nothing. She didn't keep a single thing down here. Once, she had thought about collecting an object from each human she'd turned into a meal, but she didn't truly care about such trinkets. Instead, she engraved the ceiling above with a mark after each kill. She would add another line in the morning, seeing as she was too tired and relaxed now.

Irin flicked her tail, letting it separate and shape back into her scaled iridescent legs.

Closing her eyes, Irin reflected about the kills she had made over the years and wondered what they had felt in their final moments of life.

Crackling rocks sounded from outside Irin's cave and she peeled herself from her sandy bed. She had only woken to etch her kill in the ceiling, then laid back down to count each mark. Even though she knew how many were there.

Baring her teeth into a vicious grin, she kicked her legs and swam out of her cave. A scuffle brewed, farther away, between a salmon that was becoming another creature's prey. The fish scattered as Irin slipped out from her home, but she easily caught a dark-colored one. Bringing it to her mouth, she tore into the fish, its blood and meaty flesh filling her.

Fish were foolish creatures and they should have remembered she was a predator. Her appetite rarely stayed satiated for long.

A shadow cast down above her and she peered up as a boat slowly skimmed the top of the lake. Irin ran her tongue along her teeth. She had promised herself she wouldn't go to the surface for a while, but her body itched to go above. Curious. Hungry.

Kicking her feet, Irin slowly swam upward and broke the surface without a single sound. A small fishing boat bobbed on the water with no one in sight. But then a man stood, his back turning, and placed bait on his fish hook before picking up a net. He tossed the net into the water and returned to his fishing pole.

Wavy blond hair brushed the man's tan shoulders, and the sun highlighted his bare muscular arms and back, his pants hanging low on his hips.

Irin licked her lips. Delectable. In more ways than one.

Bringing her arm up, she slammed her hand against the water before disappearing beneath the surface. Toying with her prey was a pastime she enjoyed.

Irin glided beneath the lake's warmth to the opposite side of the boat and rose from the water. With a loud cluck of the tongue, she waited for the human to rush in her direction.

The man's feet echoed when he bounded in her direction, his body leaning over the side of the boat. As the man's bright blue eyes met hers, they widened in surprise. She gave him a closed-lipped smile, not wanting him to see her fangs just yet. His gaze roamed over her iridescent flesh, the silvery scales on the sides of her face and neck, along her shoulders.

"Mermaid," he whispered.

Irin shook her head and continued to smile. Although she could turn into one, she was not a mermaid. She was only a creature of the lake.

Prying herself from the water, she climbed aboard the man's boat. He stood frozen, and she didn't miss the way his eyes trailed down her naked form. They always did. But sometimes the men or women would lunge at her, others fell to their knees, yet this man didn't do anything. Only remained there as if waiting for her to vanish from his sight. She wanted to take him right there.

"You should go," the man said in a rush.

Her brow furrowed. Go? No one had ever told her to leave before. They had either wanted to haul Irin back to shore and show her off to the village, or bring her to their home and keep her.

She shook her head no.

"I know how the world works, and they would use you to their advantage," the man said softly, taking a step

126

closer.

They would. They would either keep Irin locked in a tank or dissect her. She knew this specifically because she had been told once when a sailor had attempted to yank her to his boat's deck by her neck. Before he could pursue anything further, she had ripped off his arm and ate it in front of him as he screamed.

She shrugged at the appetizing man.

"Do you have a name? I'm Collin."

Irin nodded, then pointed at her throat. She understood the language of humans, but she couldn't speak.

"Ah, I understand. Take a seat and let me get you a few things." Collin smiled warmly.

She waited for him to grab a spear or another weapon, but instead he collected a bag from the other side of the boat. He removed a blanket and wrapped it around her shoulders, then handed her a piece of fruit.

She studied its rounded purple form and stuck out her tongue.

Collin pressed a fist to his mouth and chuckled. "You don't like fruit?"

With a shake of the head, she remembered their too sweet flavor. She had taken every variety from sailors over the years and she loathed them all.

From his pack, he pulled out a thick slice of jerky. She wrinkled her nose but plucked it from him. It appeared different than the ones she had tried before so she took a bite. A bitter taste filled her mouth and she spat it out beside Collin's bare foot.

He watched her with wide eyes and handed her a bottle. "Drink some water at least. Unless you hate that too."

That was something she wouldn't deny. Beneath the lake's surface, Irin relished gulping down water. But drinking it straight from a human's container was always better. As she drained the bottle dry, she glanced up at the darkening sky and stood to leave, her appetite gone.

"Maybe I'll see you tomorrow morning?" Collin asked as she dropped the blanket to the deck and peered down at the lake.

Without looking back, she smiled and dove into the water, wondering why she hadn't killed him. She had never done anything like this before.

Irin awoke early the next day, venturing to the middle of the lake to wait for Collin to return. This time, she told herself she would kill him, but something inside her wanted to learn more about him.

When a shadow of a boat slid over the water, a rush of giddiness formed in her chest. With a smile, she swam toward the surface.

As she pushed through the liquid, her gaze found Collin, his hands resting on the edge of his boat. A grin spread across his handsome face when his gaze met hers.

"Do you like cooked lamb?" he asked. "I brought some. Maybe you won't spit it out this time." A deep chuckle escaped his well-formed lips.

Cooked… Irin drew herself up, Collin's callused hands grasping her arms as he helped her into the boat. No one had ever done this with her—she had never allowed it, but she liked the touch of his warm hands on her flesh.

Same as before, he wrapped the blanket around her

shoulders, then brought her a plate with browned juicy meat. He cut it into thin slivers and pushed one inside her mouth, her tongue brushing the flesh of his finger. The meat was warm and bland, but she ate it anyway, all while thinking about the feel of his finger in her mouth.

Day after day, Collin brought different meats for Irin and she listened about his life, about him. The fishing store he owned, the sea paintings he loved to create. They were slowly becoming … friends? He lived alone and something about that made Irin's heart swim with joy. But not once did he ever try to bring her to shore, or kiss her. Even though her body wanted to press to his with his clothing barrier gone.

"I thought we'd paint today." He smiled. "If you want to, that is."

Irin studied the blank canvases and the assorted paints. She nodded with a grin, her fingers itching to dip into the liquid. While Collin painted the lake and its mountains using a brush, Irin created a multitude of colors with her fingertips.

He gave her another warm smile as he peered down at her canvas. "It's beautiful."

After Irin left Collin and ventured back into the lake to her cave, she stared up at her markings. For the first time in her life, Irin didn't sleep—she thought only of Collin, his full lips, his deep voice, his kindness.

129

Irin took the last bite of flesh, blood pooling in the water around her. The shark had put up quite a fight but not long enough to exhaust her. No matter the size, Irin would always defeat her prey.

As a boat's shadow drifted above, she grinned and swam past a school of trout to meet Collin.

After he helped pull her into his boat, Irin couldn't hold it in any longer. When he leaned forward to wrap the blanket around her, she pressed her lips to his. A spark spread through her at the touch.

Collin didn't hesitate as he kissed her in return, then, a moment later, pulled back, his hand nervously raking his hair. "I haven't been coming here just so I could make love to you in my boat. Please don't think that."

Irin's grin grew wider, and she leaned forward again, making it clear for him that she understood he wasn't taking advantage of her. Her lips captured his, claiming. She slanted her mouth over his, and he matched her pace.

"I've wanted you for so long," Collin whispered into her ear, making her shiver.

In answer, she peeled his shirt over his head before she lowered him to the deck. Her fingers brushed the button of his pants, and he unfastened it as she yanked them down.

He drew her closer, about to roll her to her back, but she didn't let him. Even though she trusted him, she still needed to have a chance for escape.

Heart pounding, she trailed her fingers down his cheek, his chest, then sank down on him with a silent growl, letting him fill her completely. She moved on top of him, increasing her pace as he tilted his head back and groaned. His eyes stayed shut while he gripped her hips, trusting her with *everything*.

When the pleasure washed over her and he spilled his seed inside of her, Irin knew she would remember this moment for all eternity.

She continued to meet Collin each day after that, their time filled with bliss she had never known, her skin against his, their lips locked together, their tongues tasting every warm inch of the other's body.

But she knew it couldn't last.

She was immortal.

And he was not.

Irin could have him now, but *now* was a fleeting moment—his entire *life* but a mere instant compared to hers. Her memories of him would have to be enough.

As Irin lifted off him, their bodies slick with sweat, pleasure and something far deeper consuming her, she knew Collin would do anything to protect her. How he would waste his life visiting her at the lake. She couldn't let him do that. And she couldn't let him go home and find a mortal female either. He was hers now, and hers alone.

Collin opened his arms to hold her, trusting her. His sweet eyes, his caring heart. Her smile mirrored his as she pressed a kiss to his soft lips, tasting him, remembering. And then Irin drove her fangs into his flesh, tearing open his throat, his blood pooling into her mouth, his flavor on her tongue. Collin coughed, his eyes wide, full of confusion, disbelief. Not once did he fight her, even as his breaths turned ragged. He opened his mouth to speak, but no words slipped out. Irin cradled his cheek, knowing this was the right decision as life slowly slipped from him, spilling further with each heartbeat. And then the light in his eyes was gone, and he stared blankly up at the darkening sky.

Irin wouldn't eat him like she had the others. Because he was *nothing* like them. She pried Collin from the boat and drew his body down beneath the lake where he would remain with her forever, sleeping beside her, even when he became nothing but bones.

Thorna

"*I* see a lot of you in this story, Thorna," Pyrka said, his expression soft as he studied her. "Although, I don't think you would kill your mortal love."

Even though Irin from Thorna's story would be considered monstrous by most, there was still something human about her. The not wanting things to change when they seemed perfect. Yet perfect didn't truly exist.

"No, not unless he betrayed me." She patted Pyrka's head. "Drink some blood. You've been working all day with the thorns, barely taking any sips for yourself."

"If you insist, my queen."

Thorna surveyed the butterflies and the cocoons waiting to be hatched. Any day now, a fresh batch would fill her palace, and the thought warmed her.

Whirling around, Thorna transformed to moth and left her home. A crispness permeated the chilly fall air, and a tinge of nervousness rushed through her as she drifted higher above the trees. In her younger years, she would stay a moth for days, spend the time flying, being free. That was until the beasties had crowned her as their queen.

When Asher's home slipped into view, Thorna's heart deflated a little. His old truck wasn't in his driveway, and she had thought he would have been waiting on the porch again. Perhaps he was getting tired of the stories. But he wouldn't have known she was bringing another.

Once she arrived on his porch, Thorna shifted, her dark cloak billowing from the wind. With a sigh, she fished out her favorite story of them all and she hoped he would understand what she was trying to say by leaving these gifts. Rolled inside the scroll was another letter, asking him to meet her tomorrow night—he would now know the stories were from her. She then placed her last thorned twig on top of the tale before leaving. The night's sounds sang to her as she glided through the air, and she listened to each note, each pitch, from the wind, the animals, the city. And she hoped Asher would understand her monstrous side when he learned she wasn't human.

"How do you feel about monsters?" Thorna asked, opening a new box with antique teacups covered in various prints.

Asher knelt beside her, his enticing soapy scent enveloping her. He drew out a black teacup sprinkled with thorned white roses. "I've never met one."

"What would you do if you did?"

"I don't know." Asher bit his lip, angling closer to her. He handed her the thorned teacup as a gift while he said, "What would they do if they met me? I suppose humans would be considered monsters to them."

And in that sentence, that was the precise moment when Thorna fell in love with him.

Mirror, Mirror

*S*even. *Six. Five. Four. Three. Two. One.*

Killian counted backward as Clove pressed her delicate fingertips to his closed eyelids. Seven had always been his lucky number. Always. Seven o'clock on the seventh day of the seventh month of the year 1887 was when he had married *her*.

"Eyes are the window to the soul," Clove whispered as those perfect fingers of hers drifted to his ears, her touch like silk, sending tingles down his spine. "Ears are the portal to the mind." Her fingers trailed sparks to his lips, and his breathing hitched. "And the mouth is the doorway to the body."

Killian's heart pounded while Clove's fingers traced his neck, sliding down his bare chest, over his abdomen, heat building within him, lighting a crackling fire.

He finally opened his eyes as her hand gripped him between his legs. Clove's gaze met his, her features soft, her lips crimson and plump, her raven hair falling to her waist against creamy pale skin. He wanted to kiss every single inch of her naked flesh right then, run his tongue across each curve, but her eyes danced, letting him know that would have to come later.

"And the mouth can also do wicked, wicked things," Clove murmured, her warm brown eyes still latched onto his. "Like this." She pressed her lips to his throat, giving him an open-mouth kiss. "And this." Her voice was husky as her hot mouth reached the center of his chest. Then her tongue flicked the sensitive area, and Killian shivered. "Oh, and certainly this."

And then, he was in her mouth, her tongue doing things he had never dreamed of, had never experienced with any of his past lovers before his wife. He released a deep groan as the woman he loved, his one good thing in this world, showed him how much she loved him too.

Clove stopped.

As she clutched the side of her head, she went into a coughing spell.

"Clove? Are you all right?" Killian rushed the words out, grabbing her by the shoulders. When she didn't respond, he shouted, "Clove!"

"It's my head again," she said, her voice strained while she swayed.

He scooped her up in his arms, bringing her naked body to his chest. As she glanced up, bright crimson spilled from her nose, over her ruby lips. The warmth of her blood ran down the front of him, but he ignored it.

"We're going to see the doctor, Clove."

"No," she said, her voice serious. "Every time we go, he keeps giving me medicines that do nothing except make me feel more ill."

"Please. We need to see if there's something else he can do." Richard was the only doctor in their village, and Killian trusted him.

He lowered her to the wooden floor and grabbed a rumpled old shirt for her to hold to her nose. Killian then picked up her dress that lay crumpled on the floor and helped her put it on. He fastened each button as quickly as he could before throwing on his long sleeve shirt and trousers, leaving his vest behind.

"I can walk," she said, stumbling, her face paling further.

"I know you could, but let's not try that now." Killian didn't wait for her to argue—he lifted her once more and cradled her close. Clove's breaths grew ragged as he carried her out of their small cottage and into the warm sunlight of the afternoon.

In that moment, he knew Clove's sickness was becoming worse. The episodes had been occurring for the past three months. When she had these spells, she told him she couldn't think clearly, that her words remained trapped in her throat. The last time they had gone to visit Richard, he had told them to keep what was happening to themselves. Villagers tended to whisper to one another, and sometimes malicious gossip made things worse. Killian didn't believe in witchcraft or the supernatural or anything of that nature. He only believed in Clove.

Over the past few weeks, her body had become more frail, her dresses hanging looser on her thin frame with each passing day. They were both twenty-five years of age—she was much too young for this.

A gentle breeze rumpled Killian's hair and he peered down at Clove, her eyes shut. For the moment, the blood only seeped out from her nose and not her ears or mouth as it had the last time.

The medicine may not have helped, but at least she was able to rest with it. On the nights Clove couldn't sleep, she would get up and pace back and forth in their craft room, saying it helped the blood stay in her veins.

Their chickens squawked and pecked at the ground in front of the house. The other animals were in the barn being just as loud. Killian liked that he had built their home a short distance from the other villagers, close enough they could go when things were needed, but far enough away so he and his wife could keep to themselves.

"Killian, I'm fine," Clove rasped. "It's gone now." Yet when she looked up at him, her eyes rolled back in her head and blood seeped from her ears.

Damn it. Killian ran, holding his wife close as he passed through the trees and over fallen limbs into the village. Wooden and stone houses slipped into view, and smoke billowed out of the chimneys of several. In the distance, children's laughter echoed. It was a Sunday, and after church service had ended, most everyone stayed in their homes and did what they could to make up for their sins.

Richard's home was on the very edge of the village, so Killian wouldn't have to carry Clove much farther. As he walked up the creaking steps of Richard's porch, Killian glanced at the single fern that was always there. Lifting his fist, Killian banged on the door, not once stopping until Richard pulled it open.

"What are you doing, Killian?" The doctor frowned, his glasses sliding down his nose, and his gray hair disheveled. Richard's gaze fell to Clove and he waved them in. "Hurry, bring her to the table."

Richard's home was neat and tidy, and he lived alone. His wife had passed a few years prior from an illness that had taken almost half of the village, which might have been why Richard continued to put extra effort into helping Clove. Richard knew what it was like to lose someone he loved—he kept the lone fern on his porch because it had been his wife's favorite.

Clove shivered, peering at them, seeming too tired to speak at the moment. Her eyes closed, her breaths became even, and Killian knew she had fallen asleep. The bleeding appeared to have stopped, and he relaxed a fraction. He lowered his wife, careful not to disturb her, onto the doctor's table and took a step back to leave Richard enough room to help her.

Richard pressed his stethoscope to Clove's chest and took a listen. "Her heart still sounds healthy." He cleaned the blood from her face with a wet rag, then placed a wrinkled hand to her forehead. "Temperature isn't high. But by looking at her, I know something is wrong." Richard studied Killian as though he was warring with himself about something. "You don't know yet, do you?"

Killian furrowed his brow. "Know what?"

"She's carrying your child."

Everything within him stilled. "Child?"

"She came to me a few days ago. I know it's not my place to tell you, but I would want to know if it was my wife." Richard paused and changed the subject as if he hadn't just confessed this news. "Let's try something else this time."

Richard left Clove and headed to a small cabinet across the room while Killian's mind spun.

A child? They had discussed children before, but neither had been ready. As he thought about a boy with Clove's dark hair or a girl with her deep brown eyes, he couldn't help but smile. But then he thought about how weak she had become, and he didn't know if she would truly be able to carry a child to full term.

He clasped Clove's clammy hand while Richard moved around several glass jars. Richard took two small ones, along with a bundle of sage—twine wrapped around the herb's middle.

Killian frowned at the bundle. "Why do we need

sage?”

“It’s said it keeps the Devil away.”

Killian didn’t believe in the Devil, but he kept his lips sealed, trying to stay polite. Any talk of that would be blasphemy, and he wouldn’t risk the villagers gossiping about Clove. His wife believed in all those things, though—Heaven, Hell, God, the Devil, angels, demons. Because of her beliefs, he would burn the sage for her.

After accepting the items, Killian reached into his pocket to draw out payment.

Richard stopped him with a hand on his arm. “Not today. It’s on me. I’ll pray for her tonight, as I do every night. And I’ll pray for the child growing in her belly.”

“Thank you,” Killian said, not believing in prayers, either. Why would he? They had never been answered in his past. Not when his sister died, not when his twin brother died, not when his parents died, nor when Clove’s parents died. His aunt and uncle still lived in the village, but he rarely spoke to them.

“Remember, don’t say anything about what she’s facing to anyone,” Richard said.

“I won’t.” Killian lifted Clove from the table, her eyes remaining shut, her breathing still even.

As she slept in his arms, he slowly walked back through the forest, careful not to jostle her too much.

The chickens lifted their heads when Killian passed them, as though sensing something was wrong. Clove went outside every morning and spent long hours with the animals, especially the chickens and goats. She would read her Bible, sew, or dance in circles with her hair down, rain or shine.

Killian opened the door and set Clove on the bed in their room. A small squeak escaped her mouth, but she didn't stir.

He then went into their craft room and tossed the sage on his desk before sinking into his chair. He glanced at himself in the mirror hanging on the wall, noticing the heavy bags beneath his green eyes. His thoughts turned to his wife. Ever since their childhood, Clove had been a free spirit, but it wasn't until they were twelve that a deep friendship formed between them. He hadn't loved her at first—he was stupid then. For years he didn't see it, until one day it had hit him all at once.

Clove still had her whole life in front of her, and she was fighting not only for herself, but their child. He would burn the sage that night, yet for now, he would pray for her, even though it had never helped him before. "I will do anything for her to live. I would sacrifice myself for her. I need my wife to be all right. Please."

"Do you now?" a deep voice whispered.

Killian whirled around and stood, his wide eyes searching the room for where the voice had come from. He grabbed his rifle from his desk. But no one was there.

"You want to know what is truly wrong with your wife, do you not?" the male voice purred.

Killian glanced toward the mirror, where the voice seemed to have come from this time. Yet only Killian's image reflected back at him. The oval mirror looked the same as it always did, ordinary—a bronze leafy pattern framed its clear glass. The antique had belonged to his parents, which had been handed down for generations. There had never been anything unusual about it before, but it was no ordinary mirror now.

He reached for the sage, preparing to light it, when the mirror spoke. "That is not going to do anything." The male voice had clearly come from the mirror, but no face appeared.

"Who are you?" Killian asked, inching closer with his rifle raised.

"You called on me, did you not?" the mirror cooed. "You want your precious love to heal. I can help you with that."

"A devil would never speak the truth."

"Her illness cannot be cured by a human. She will die before winter comes."

Killian's hands shook as he lowered his rifle a fraction. His wife… Their child… "I will not let her die."

"Then you will have to trust me." The voice paused. "Grab her handheld mirror from her sewing desk and break it."

Furrowing his brow, Killian stared at the mirror, trying to see the face beyond the glass. "That is devil tricks."

"Fine, then do not believe me."

Killian clenched his teeth and tightened his fists to stop from trembling. He didn't quite believe what this being was saying, but he knew with his whole heart that his love was dying. And that she would die while carrying their child.

At the moment, Killian wasn't sure if he was dreaming or if he was awake, but he decided that if his wife could be healed, he would believe anything—he would dream forever. He set the rifle on the table and lifted Clove's silver mirror, then slammed it against the desk with a crash, shattering its glass, shards falling against the wooden floor.

Something tugged at Killian. It wasn't pain—it was as if some unknown, invisible force was pulling at his body. In an instant, his feet left the floor, and he was no longer in his home. He now stood directly across from the Devil himself in a room of mirrored walls.

Killian's mother had always been superstitious, saying that breaking a mirror would bring seven years of bad luck. He hadn't believed in any of her superstitions, and if Clove died, he would already be getting more than seven years of bad luck anyway.

He sucked in a sharp breath as he studied the man—no, not a man, but something else—before him in a warm room filled with mirror walls, floor, and ceiling. The male stood tall, staring back at him with irises of silver. Two small pointed horns that appeared to be mirror glass rested on his forehead. His lips were a pale blue, white hair hung to his waist, and pearlescent scales covered his body. The only clothing he wore on his lean and toned form was a pair of tight dark leather pants—even his feet were bare.

Perhaps the Devil does exist.

"Where am I? What did you *do*?" Killian demanded, clenching his fists so they wouldn't shake. "You're the Devil, aren't you?"

The male's lips twitched, and Killian's gaze drifted back to the stranger's horns, where his own desperate image reflected.

"I am a demon," the male finally said, "but I am not the Devil you speak of. He is in another place and would not provide you the opportunity that I am. Humans go to him. I do not collect them here. You are in Veidrodis." His eyes sparked, the silver in them shining as though

143

they were made from glass too.

"You said you would help Clove," Killian said through gritted teeth. "You lied!"

"I did no such thing." The demon sauntered forward. "And you may call me Nuodėmė. I will help you save your wife. That is no lie. But you will have to complete several tasks for me first. Something of this nature will not come without payment."

Nuodėmė had only said the word tasks, but Killian knew it wouldn't be something as simple as cleaning the mirrors in this room. A demon shouldn't be trusted so easily, but Killian was curious, desperate. "What do you want me to do?"

"A couple of things today. A couple tomorrow. Two more on day three. A final task on the fourth day. Then your wife will be saved."

Four days. Killian would only have to be here four days, but did time here work the same? Four days here could be twenty years at home. It would be bad enough to leave Clove in her condition for a short period, but any longer than that… "Four days, in my world?"

"Yes."

Then, if what the demon spoke was true, Clove would live. He couldn't let hope seep in just yet, not until she was no longer sick. But … there was a chance.

Killian nodded and glanced behind him, finding the wall held an oval mirror that matched the one in the craft room. Its glass reflected Clove's rocking chair.

Nuodėmė cleared his throat and Killian turned to face him. "If you prefer to do nothing, I can leave." The demon arched a brow.

"I'll do it."

Nuodėmė motioned him to follow, and with a wave

of his hand, a door within the mirror wall slid open.

Killian swallowed the lump in his throat, his heart slamming against his rib cage as his gaze studied the new room in its entirety. Males and females, not the least bit human, filled the large space, each one appearing different than the other. Some with tails, their bodies the size of humans or small dolls, others the size of giants, their massive heads nearly touching the room's high-vaulted ceiling. Scales covered several, fur others. Their skin colors all varied, but the one thing they had in common was the mirror horns protruding from their foreheads. Even then, those were different too.

The couple nearest Killian lazily sipped from their silver goblets, and the female wiped a streak of red from her chin that looked suspiciously like blood. A shirtless demon relaxed on a chaise, his eyes closed, his head tipped back while a female wearing a corset and a male in a loincloth fed him grapes.

Killian had never seen such sin in his life. Naked bodies were mounted atop one another throughout the entire room. On one side, a female straddled a male, rocking her hips forward, her back arching. In a corner, a muscular male thrust into a tall male demon against the wall. On the other side, two females joined another male. He gripped one's neck and kissed her wickedly while the other performed a different kind of kissing between his thighs. His village would yell blasphemy, but Killian would only call it pleasure, just as he would when he and Clove would do acts of sin with their own bodies.

The floor was the same glass as in the room he had come from, except ornate rugs scattered across its length. Thousands of glass lanterns hung from the enormous mirror ceiling, the silvery flames within them shining like stars, reflecting to infinity along the ceiling, walls, and floor between the rugs.

As if sensing Killian staring, the demons turned their heads and focused on him. No, not him—their king. In that moment, Killian knew that this demon was not an ordinary demon—he was king of this Veidrodis.

"Enough gawking," Nuodėmė said to the demons. "Carry on with your pleasuring."

They bowed their heads and returned to their activities.

Before Killian could speak, the demon king continued, "On Sundays, I allow everyone to come in here and get their fill of gratification." He paused. "Now, for your two tasks. I want you to steal a bowl of grapes from someone, then go back to your room and eat them all."

Killian frowned, not understanding what sort of tasks these were. This demon king who had brought him here wanted him to eat a bowl full of *grapes*? It was simple, almost *too* simple. "What if I'm not hungry?"

"Then say goodbye to your wife." Nuodėmė shrugged and bared his teeth so Killian could see the back ones came to sharp points.

"I'll do it," Killian answered.

"Go on." The demon king flicked his wrist in the air. "I won't come to you again until tomorrow." Nuodėmė spun on his heels and arrogantly strutted to his obsidian throne, where he lowered himself with the grace of a great stag. The demon king's chin lifted, his silvery gaze scanning the room, seeming to look for someone. He unfastened his pants, and the female he must have been searching for swayed her hips as she approached him, then sank to her knees and performed her duty to the demon king.

It took Killian longer than he wanted to remove his gaze from what he was seeing. This was madness. But he needed to do only these two tasks that would get him two steps closer to saving Clove. Or, at least, he hoped it truly would.

Killian's gaze settled on a glass bowl filled with deep purple grapes, resting beside two kissing females.

A female demon, wearing furs that barely covered her breasts and a skirt which left most of her legs on display, slid beside him. Her chestnut-colored hair fell in waves against pale violet skin. "Are you sure that is the one you want to choose?"

He inspected each dish around the room—glass bowls, purple grapes. "They all look the same."

She shrugged, her expression unreadable. "Perhaps, or perhaps not."

"Well, which is it?"

She furrowed her brow and walked away, leaving Killian reconsidering what he was going to do. But then again, a demon would lie.

Thinking of Clove and what her Bible said about the lies demons had spilled, he snatched the bowl of fruit. Before heading back to his empty and windowless room, Killian's gaze locked on Nuodėmė, who watched him with a smirk on his face as he was getting pleasured.

Scowling, Killian walked into the room and the door slid shut behind him.

Taking a plump grape, he tossed it into his mouth, tasting its sweetness as he chewed. Killian took another and another, growing more ravenous. With each taste, the flavor only got better, and he peered down, knowing they would be nearly gone by now.

However, they weren't. The bowl was just as full as it had been. His eyes widened as he took a handful, plopping one after the other into his mouth. But the bowl never emptied.

As he continued to eat, the flavor of the grapes soured his stomach, yet he forced himself to keep going.

A panic stirred within him when there didn't seem to be an end for the fruit. How was he supposed to finish a bowl of grapes if there was no end to them?

But still, he pressed on, gorging himself, shoving them into his mouth, faster and faster, nearly choking, until nausea threatened to undo his task. Terror filled him at the thought, and Killian froze, swallowing, forcing the bile back. He closed his eyes and took a deep breath, steadying his trembling nerves. *I must complete this task and save Clove.*

And so, for the rest of the night, Killian continued to eat the fruit. Slowly … methodically...

When he felt as though his stomach would burst, the blasted grapes finally started to lessen in their bowl, until he shoved the last one into his mouth. His eyelids grew heavy, but he wouldn't allow himself to sleep on the floor. If he did that, it would put him in an even more vulnerable position in this place. So he relaxed his back against the glass and shut his eyes, still in a position that would be easy to rise from and defend himself if needed. Though, even if he had his rifle in hand, he knew it wouldn't kill a demon. There was nothing he could truly do against Nuodėmė and his world of demons.

An ear-piercing scream stirred Killian from his sleep, and he jumped to his feet.

"No, no, no. Wake up, Killian!" Clove cried.

It was her, her voice, coming from the other side of the mirror leading to his room. He ran to the glass and found Clove cradling someone's upper body in her lap. Tears spilled down her cheeks as she continued to tell the man to wake up. *Him*. The body she was holding and talking to was *him*. How? He was standing right here in this demon world.

"Clove!" Killian shouted, though he was certain she wouldn't hear him.

But then she gasped and peered down at his body. "Killian?" Her face fell again when the body didn't rouse.

Yet, she had heard him.

"Clove! I'm right here in the mirror." Even to himself, it sounded mad, but as her gaze met the glass, he wondered if she could see him.

Her lips parted and she gently moved his body from her lap. Slowly, hesitantly, she walked to the mirror. Her face held an emotion that seemed to be telling him she didn't know if she should trust what she was hearing.

"Killian?" she finally said, her eyes squinting at the glass.

"Yes, my lucky clover," he whispered. "Can you see me?"

Her eyes widened. "I-I don't see you in the mirror."

"I'm here, Clove."

"You're a ghost, then?" Tears rained down her cheeks as she took a step back, her hands cupping her mouth. Killian wanted to reach his hand through the glass and wipe her tears away. He wanted to draw her close so he could feel her warmth, so she could feel his.

"I don't know why my body is there. But I'm alive. I know this doesn't make sense, but I will come back in a few days." Again, he hoped he would.

"I don't understand, Killian," she whispered. "Perhaps I'm mad and imagining all of this in my grief."

"I swear to you I'm not dead. I struck a deal with someone who can help us save you. Someone otherworldly." He wouldn't confess to her that it was a demon because he knew how deep her faith went. She would tell him he was a fool and not to listen to any of them. "I know it's hard to accept, but please believe me."

"I don't know what to believe," she murmured.

"Leave my body there for now. I don't know how often I'll be able to speak to you. But I'll come back. I promise. I'm going to save you, Clove, along with our child."

She gasped. "You know? I was going to tell you, but I didn't know when. Not with everything happening."

"I know, and we will get through this, all right?" Even though his words sounded true, he didn't believe them fully. Not yet.

"Please, watch over yourself. If what you say is true, and I'm not imagining this, don't trust anyone except for yourself. I need you here, Killian."

He placed his hand against the cool glass, wishing he could press it through to lace his fingers with hers. "Put your palm to the mirror."

Shakily, she lifted her hand and rested it on the glass. He trailed his palm across the mirror—it was so close to connecting to hers, only a thin line of hardness separating them from one another.

"I know you don't feel this," he said in a soft voice. "But I'm touching you, holding you, kissing you, loving you.”

“I love—” Her hand slipped from the glass as a coughing spell erupted from her throat, blood splattering the mirror. Crimson then flooded out from her nose.

“Clove!” Killian shouted.

She didn’t seem to hear him as she stumbled backward and collapsed on the floor. Her eyes fluttered shut while her chest slowly rose and fell. In that moment, he couldn’t do anything to help her.

Yet, he would do anything to save her. He already was.

The mirror door behind Killian slid open, and he whirled around to find Nuodėmė leaning against the frame, the demon king’s arms crossed. Ignoring Nuodėmė, Killian turned back to face his wife.

“Clove!” he screamed, pounding the glass.

“I’m all right,” his wife whispered, but she clearly wasn’t. She pushed herself from the floor and sank onto her rocking chair.

“Do you want to spend all day speaking to a dying woman through the glass?” Nuodėmė purred. “Or do you want to fulfill your tasks and go home to your body?”

Killian scowled. “I’m not leaving her alone.” Not when she was like this.

“Your choice.” Nuodėmė’s lips twitched.

Resigned, Killian’s shoulders slumped, and he knew he couldn’t linger in this room all morning—speaking to his wife through the glass—if he wanted to save her.

“I have to go for now, Clove,” he said. “I promise I’ll

be back." *Soon*. He would come back to her soon.

"Killian, what's happening?" she asked, a nervous edge laced in her words. "Killian, what foolishness are you *doing*?"

He had never ignored her before, not once. But he had to in this moment—otherwise, he wouldn't find the courage to leave this room, to leave her.

And so Killian turned his back on his wife and went to the demon king. "What's your prize for all of this? Why are you helping us?"

"Mmm." Nuodėmė rubbed at his scaled jaw, his silvery gaze dancing with amusement. "Perhaps I like feeding off your misery. Enjoy the grapes?"

That wasn't a satisfying answer, but the demon king wasn't going to give a direct one anyhow. "I did," Killian said through gritted teeth, recalling the alluring flavor of the plump fruit at first. Then how the taste had soured his stomach as he was forced to eat more and more and *more*. The female demon had warned him about that bowl of fruit, yet he had chosen not to listen. But it was over now. The grapes, all thousands of them, were in his stomach.

Nuodėmė chuckled. "Clove is special, is she not?"

Killian didn't answer. The demon king didn't need to know more about his wife than he already did. But Nuodėmė most likely knew everything about them both since the bastard was a demon.

Nuodėmė led him into the throne room, and this time it was cleared out. The settees were empty, not a single demon or bowl of fruit in sight.

"Where is everyone?" Killian asked, trailing a finger across the back of a soft velvet settee.

"They are not needed at the moment." Nuodėmė's lips curled into a vicious smile. "Or perhaps, one is. I want you to go into a room down the hall and pierce a demon's heart, then return here for your next task."

Horror twisted in Killian's gut. Eating an endless bowl of grapes was one thing, but murdering someone? "I can't," he stuttered.

"You will or you won't." Nuodėmė drew a dagger from his waist. The light from above reflected off the weapon's surface. It was made entirely of silvery glass. "The way to end a demon is by piercing them with mirror glass."

Killian thought about ripping the blade from Nuodėmė's hand and shoving it through his heart. But how would that save his wife?

Almost every day, back at home, Killian went hunting. Sometimes Clove came with him and they would track down deer, rabbits, and birds. Other times, he would slaughter their pigs and chickens when their lives had run their course. After each kill, Clove would say a prayer for the animals. She believed not only did humans enter Heaven or Hell, but animals did too.

A demon wasn't a human, but that didn't make the task any easier. He would have to think of it as if he was going on a hunt, as though it was necessary.

"Fine." Killian took the blade from Nuodėmė's hand and held it tight. It was practically weightless, its surface cool to the touch. "Any demon will do?"

"One from any of the rooms down the hall. My brother, Kosmaras, has them all in a deep sleep. They may be having a nightmare or two at the moment... Kosmaras does not stay here, though. He is in his own realm of nightmares." The demon king chuckled, flicking his hand in the air and sauntering toward his throne.

Clutching the dagger close, Killian left the room and

entered a long hallway filled with silvery doors. As his boots thumped against the glass, he froze, terror threatening to overtake him at last. The walls appeared to be mirrors, the same as the others, but this time his reflections moved on their own, dozens upon dozens of Killians, trapped, pounding soundlessly on the glass—surrounding him on all sides, above his head and below his feet—their mouths moving in silent pleas for him to turn back.

Killian's heart quickened, his throat tight when he swallowed. Sweat beaded his brow as he ignored the images and passed door after door, not knowing which to choose. But did it matter? He could choose any of them. A part of Killian begged him to listen to the moving reflections, but he couldn't.

He stopped in front of a door, wondering what sinister hell lay inside. But it appeared no different than the other entrances, so he grabbed the glass handle, his chest heaving. Turning it, he opened the door to silence.

Darkness bathed the room in its entirety, his heart pounding harder as he entered. He couldn't see a damn thing and was about to choose another room, which could potentially be worse, when the glass blade he held began to glow, casting a silvery light. He lifted it in front of him, its glow illuminating a fur rug sprawled across the floor, a looming wardrobe against a wall, then his eyes widened as they settled on something in the center of the room.

Killian pressed forward, shining the blade's light on a coffin made of the same mirror glass as almost everything else here. For once, he wished the glass of the coffin was clear so he could see straight into it, see what rested inside.

As he crept closer to what had to be the demon's bed,

Killian shakily pressed a hand to the cool glass. He then lifted the lid, another spell of quiet enveloping him, not a single groan or squeak.

A rosewood scent struck his nose as his trembling hand raised the dagger forward. Inside, a male demon, with small glass horns similar to Nuodėmė's, slept. His thick eyelashes rested against ivory-furred cheeks, and dark hair cascaded down his naked chest. The demon was more pretty than masculine. His eyes moved behind his closed lids as though he was trapped in a nightmare and unable to wake himself. Killian recalled the words about Nuodėmė's brother, Kosmaras. He wondered if it would be worse to strike a deal with that demon.

Shakily, he brought both hands to the dagger's hilt and hovered over the male's chest. He thought of Clove's lovely face, begging him to stop, to not do this. For her, Killian repeated one of her prayers that she had written down and placed inside her Bible. Her Bible was full of notes, prayers, and folded pages of her favorite passages. She had never once tried to force him to believe what she did, just as he never tried to make her not believe. But in this moment, he did believe, and in this moment, he knew he was a sinner as he shoved the blade into the demon's chest, piercing his heart. Or perhaps, Killian wouldn't be punished since a demon was said to be a wicked, wicked thing. Either way, it was the choice he had made for his wife and their child.

The demon didn't scream, didn't even open his eyes, only his lips parted on a sharp inhale before his chest stopped rising.

As liquid pooled out from the demon's wound, Killian shouldn't have been surprised by the male bleeding out bright red, but he was. It matched the color that had spilled from Clove's nose—the same red Killian had bled in the past from injuries. He wasn't sure what he had expected, but perhaps black. This made the male seem all that much more human.

Killian didn't know what to feel. Sickness thrummed in his gut as he stumbled backward and struck the wall. *What have I done*? But below the guilt, the nausea, was something else: glee. Like he had *enjoyed* doing it, even wanted to open a door to another room and do it again. Again and again.

"Stop it," Killian told himself. "Stop it. This isn't you." Nausea filled him, and he tried to expel his stomach but nothing rose to the surface—none of the grapes from the night before made a reappearance.

With a fist to his mouth, Killian ran out of the room, back down the hallway, not looking at any of his reflections—who seemed to stare at him in disapproval. But he had chosen this path and would choose it again as he thought about Clove's frail body in their craft room at home.

"Ah." Nuodėmė stood in the center of the throne room, grinning when Killian entered. "Task number three is complete. Do you want your last one for the day?"

No. No more. "Yes."

Nuodėmė slid up behind him and pressed his chest to Killian's back, the demon's breath hot on his ear while he whispered, "Watch yourself in the mirror as you cut out your eye."

Killian inhaled sharply and whirled around. "*What*?"

"I said"—Nuodėmė cocked his head and licked his lips—"remove your eye for your next task."

"Something else." He shook his head and backed up into the wall.

"You have two," the demon purred. "You will be fine."

Like hell I will be fine.

"If you choose not to, then Clove will die."

Killian's nostrils flared, but he wouldn't overthink this. It would be giving a piece of himself for his wife, not Nuodėmė.

Slowly, he peeled himself from the wall and turned to face the mirror. Killian gripped the dagger tighter in his fist as he studied himself: his green eyes, his short and curly red hair.

"Your eyes are like emeralds," Clove whispered.

He stared at himself—this time his hand didn't shake as it had with the demon. Focused, he plunged the dagger into his left eye. A sharp, agonizing pain barreled through him, tearing a scream from his throat, the air frozen in his lungs. "Fuck! Holy fuck!" The pain radiated from his eye to his skull, to *everywhere*. Warm blood spilled down Killian's cheek, but he ignored it. His breaths came out ragged while he finished cutting the eyeball out.

Nuodėmė lazily took both Killian's eye and the dagger from him. The gleam in the demon's smile seemed as though he had been gifted the finest of jewels.

"Now, return to your room. I shall see you in the morning for your next tasks." The demon king turned around and disappeared from the throne room, leaving Killian alone, trembling.

He entered his room, the door sliding shut behind him. Tightening his fists, he released a roar, spittle flying from his mouth. He screamed once more to escape the agony, both physically and emotionally. Again, he questioned what he had done, then a voice reminded him why.

"Killian!" Clove shouted, hobbling toward the mirror. Just the sound of her voice helped soothe him, even though the pain inside his eye socket burned like flames to flesh.

"I'm here," he rasped, darting toward her and placing his hand to the glass.

"Why were you screaming?" she asked, her voice tinged with fright.

"It's nothing. I'm two steps closer to seeing you again." *Three steps away from saving you.*

"How are you feeling?" He wanted to focus on her, focus away from what had just happened.

"I'm sewing a baby blanket in a room with your unmoving body beside me, so I'm doing well, it seems." She smiled, attempting to lighten the mood. But in her eyes, he could see the worry there.

Killian wouldn't trouble her now about everything he had done, but when he saw her again, he would confess to her his sins, and then she could help take them away with her prayers and kisses.

Killian opened his eye, and his gaze settled on the demon king standing across from him. "Why are you watching me sleep?" He shoved himself away from the wall to a standing position. Not once had he slipped and allowed himself the comfort of curling up on the floor. Throughout the night, Killian had thought about the demon he had slain inside his glass coffin. The pain in Killian's eye socket had faded to a dull throb that reminded him of what he had also done to himself.

"I am only waiting on you to wake," Nuodėmė cooed, pushing a lock of silky white hair over his shoulder.

"I'm awake now."

"Let us not waste time, then." Nuodėmė motioned him forward. "Now, shall we?"

Killian peered into the mirror, finding Clove still asleep in her rocking chair, a patchwork blanket wrapped around her shoulders. Her hands clutched her stomach while she slept as if protecting their child.

The day before, they had talked to each other until they could no longer hold their eyes open. Clove hadn't had any bloody spells and their chatting had felt like before, when they hadn't had any worries in the world. It had been the perfect distraction from him remembering where he was.

Killian didn't want to disturb his wife, so he pressed his hands to the glass and whispered, "I love you."

"Love..." Nuodėmė drawled.

"What of it? Do demons not love?" Killian scowled as he stepped up beside the king at the door.

"Not usually."

"Have you?" Killian asked, recalling the female who had pleasured the demon king in the throne room.

Nuodėmė smirked, then spun on his heels and the door slid open. Voices echoed from the throne room. Killian followed behind Nuodėmė, and this time the large space wasn't empty. It was as it had been the first day, filled with demons chatting, groping one another, and bowls of fruit beside them.

"What do you want me to do now?" Killian asked, his gaze settling on a small, wrinkled demon, the size of his hand, painting on a large canvas. *What do you want me to do that is worse than yesterday?*

"Sit. Relax. Enjoy."

Killian furrowed his brow. *Enjoy* what? *Tearing out another eye?*

Nuodėmė narrowed his gaze, then clucked his tongue. Killian heeded the warning and took a seat on an empty settee. He swallowed deeply as the demons around groaned and moaned, and he couldn't help but feel like a voyeur. Someone sank down next to him—it was the female from the other day who had warned him about the grapes.

"You did not listen to me," she said.

"No." He paused. "It doesn't matter—I did what he wanted."

"If I were you, I would stop now." She stared straight ahead as though she wasn't talking to him. "Do it for your wife."

"I *am* doing this for her," he whispered.

"You will not like what is next."

It didn't matter what the next task was, either—he would do it. As he glanced over to tell her just that, his body froze.

The demon was peeling off her top, her breasts exposed, her nipples pebbling. He jerked his head in the other direction, but from her movements, he knew she was removing her skirt as well.

"Fuck her," a voice whispered at his ear, breath hot.

He turned around to find Nuodėmė beside him once more, a smirk on his face.

Killian's throat bobbed as he swallowed. "No."

"Your next task is to fuck Rožė."

"I can't." He wouldn't. He would never… That was one thing he couldn't do.

And then Rožė's hand was on his knee, drifting up

his thigh. Killian's heart pounded and his chest heaved when her palm was so close to touching his manhood.

"I said *no*." He pushed himself to stand, away from Rožė.

"Ah, aren't you the little fighter?" Nuodėmė chuckled. "This one time, all right? You will not have to couple with her, but you will have to spill yourself while watching her."

Killian ran a hand down his face. That still felt wrong. So incredibly wrong. But that would be something Clove could forgive him for. If he had lain with a demon, or anyone else for that matter, it would have been unforgivable. But this he could do, and he would imagine it was his wife while watching the female.

"Fine." Killian's hands shook as he unfastened his pants and pulled himself out.

"Look at you," Nuodėmė purred. "You could please anyone here if you so choose."

Killian closed his eye, holding his anger back. If he didn't, he would find a way to slit the demon king's throat. A sinful thought. A sinful urge. But he didn't give a damn in that moment.

He opened his lid, finding Rožė standing before him, and Killian inhaled sharply. He ignored her large breasts and how she lacked curls between her violet thighs. Everything about her was different than his wife, and he didn't know if he would be able to fulfill the task—if he could get himself to spill for her and the demon king.

He kept his gaze trained on Rožė's face, only he pretended as though he was looking at his wife. His beautiful, perfect wife. Her milky skin, her long black hair, her ruby red lips. The light scar that fell across her stomach from when she had scraped it on a sharp rock in the river. He pictured her dark curls between her thighs, her small but perky breasts, her peaked nipples.

A heat spread through him then, dipping lower, straight to where he needed his hand to stroke. He did just that, staring at the demon's face, but seeing Clove in his mind. Killian focused on the times over the years when they had been flesh to flesh, him inside her. The first time he had truly noticed her, when she had leaned against a tree, watching him chop wood. She had been buried in her Bible as usual, but something in her gaze that day had told him she was looking at him as something more than a friend. Killian had brought other women in the village to his bed before that, but it had been different as he studied Clove that day. He had wanted her too.

Killian's hand continued to move as he thought about their first kiss in the river, then him worshiping her body beside the water. A few weeks later, he had asked her to be his wife, and she had said yes. He imagined Clove's lips on his, his hand between her thighs, her hand on him, then her mouth, before finally sinking onto him as his fingers dug into her hips. His wife's hips rolling and rolling until he groaned, whispering her name in a room full of demons, instead of back at home where he would hold her against his heaving chest afterward.

"Now, clean yourself up." Nuodėmė held out a red cloth.

"Is that my next task?" Killian said between gritted teeth, taking the cloth and wiping himself.

"Ah, I love your humor, my sweet. But tease like that again, and I may have you remove your other eye." Nuodėmė leaned forward, his smile turning into something dangerous. "Then how would you see your precious Clove's face?"

Killian knew when to keep quiet, and this was one of those moments. So his gaze shifted to Rožė who was now fully dressed, even though most of her flesh was still on display. As her eyes met his, there was a look on her face that seemed like she wanted to say something else. But she shifted her stare to Nuodėmė, who was watching her.

"Thank you, my king," she whispered and scurried away, leaving Killian wondering what she was afraid of. And what was her connection to Nuodėmė?

"What's my next task, then?" Killian asked, breaking the tense silence between them.

Nuodėmė took back his red cloth and tossed it on an empty settee. "I want you to go to your room and sleep until morning."

"How is that a task?" he asked, knowing he should have bitten his damn tongue before speaking the words.

"Would you rather me send you to collect the heart of a demon or have you cut out your tongue?"

Killian's eye widened. Sleep it was, then. Sleep would get him out of this forsaken room.

"I'll do it. Thank you." Even though Killian had woken not long ago and wasn't the least bit tired, he would force himself to sleep. This seemed the simplest of the tasks thus far, but … he had assumed that about the grapes. His stomach churned as he thought about the fruit, and if he did truly get back home, he would never touch one again.

"Go then," Nuodėmė turned and walked away.

With one last glance at the demon's back, Killian returned to his room. The bright light shone from the ceiling, and he wasn't sure that would help him sleep. He hurried to the mirror where he found Clove stitching a yellow and green blanket in her lap, one that could only

be for their baby. Guilt washed over him as he watched
her, knowing what he had just done in front of another
female. But he hadn't seen Rožė, not once—it had all
been his wife.

"I'm here, Clove," Killian rasped, pressing his hand
to the glass.

His wife dropped the blanket and rushed to the
mirror, a smile and worry both on her face. She placed
her palm to the glass, almost perfectly aligning with his.

"Are you holding your hand to the mirror?" Clove
asked.

"I am," he whispered. "Tomorrow, I'll hopefully
come back to you." *Hopefully*.

"Your body is stiff already, and an odor is starting to
come from it." Her voice quivered. "I don't know if
you're truly dead and I'm imagining our conversations.
What if it's because I want you to be here so much that
I'm delusional? I don't know what to do."

"Trust me," he pleaded. "Trust me that I'm not dead."
At least, he believed he wasn't… But what if the demon
had truly taken his soul to linger here forever while his
body rotted. He could just be the demon king's toy, his
plaything. *No.* He would trust that Nuodėmė wouldn't go
back on his word, regardless of what he was.

"All right, Killian," she finally said. "I will continue
to pray. So far, I haven't had any bleeding today, either."

Perhaps with each task, she was getting better. Her
skin no longer appeared an unhealthy shade of pale, and
her body didn't seem as frail.

Killian smiled. "Thank you, and that's wonderful. I'll
talk to you tomorrow."

"I love you, husband."

"I love you more, wife."

Killian's hand slipped from the mirror, his lids flickering. Tiredness swept through him, seeping into each layer of muscle, all the way down to his bones. He yawned and lowered himself to the floor, then leaned against the wall. As he closed his eye, he would dream of his wife and their child, along with the beautiful possibilities they could have together one day.

"Still asleep, human?" A booted foot kicked at Killian's leg.

His lids peeled open for a brief moment, then fluttered shut.

"Wakey, wakey," Nuodėmė said and snapped his fingers near Killian's ear.

His eye opened wide, the tiredness clearing instantly. He pushed himself to stand and felt as though he had been awake for hours with energy running through his veins. No dreams or nightmares had come to him while he slept. There had just been that—sleep and darkness.

"Is it time for my final task?" Killian asked.

"You are correct," the demon purred. "I did not say when it would be, though."

"You said the fourth day."

"I suppose we can do it now, then?" He grinned before turning on his heels and motioning Killian with a finger to follow.

Killian wasn't in the mood for Nuodėmė today, but he kept his mouth closed. One more task would allow Clove and their child to live.

He followed the demon king and headed into the

throne room. This time, it wasn't filled with demons, but it wasn't only Nuodėmė and Killian, either. A tall male wearing only fur pants, hooves for feet, and a face appearing more like a buffalo, stood there. Beside him was a familiar face with dark hair to her waist and a lacy dress hanging down her body.

Clove.

Clove was *here*.

"What if I tell you she is to die?" Nuodėmė said, not a single emotion in his voice.

Killian's heart pounded as the beastly male drew Clove to his chest, pressing a glass blade to her throat.

"Stop!" Killian shouted.

The buffalo demon gripped Clove's shoulder with his other hand, and she gasped. She tried to mouth something, but no words came out. Just like when he had gone down the mirror hallway to kill a demon. He hadn't heard his images speak that time, either. Killian couldn't read her lips while they moved, yet he strained to do so.

Killian had to find a way to get to his wife without this demon spilling her blood. Anger boiled in his veins. "Let her go, damn it!"

"How would this make you feel?" Nuodėmė asked, flicking his wrist in the air.

The buffalo male took the blade from Clove's throat and shoved it directly into her chest.

Time stopped. Everything stopped. His wife's knees buckled, and she collapsed to the floor.

Rage rose within Killian, so much so that he flung himself at the buffalo male and punched him in the face, pounding and pounding him over and over. The demon didn't fight back, just seemed to take it as Killian wrapped his hands around his fur throat and squeezed.

The rage in him wouldn't stop—it grew stronger with each passing second. He wanted to snap the male's head off.

"Enough," Nuodėmė demanded. "Look at her, and you will see."

Killian didn't want to stop—he wanted to tear the buffalo demon apart. But he willed himself to glance at Clove and stilled. It wasn't the body of his wife he was looking at, but Rožė. Her chest didn't rise, and her eyes stared blankly up at the ceiling. A rush of feelings barreled through him—relief but also pity and sadness even though he didn't know her. Yet behind all that, the lingering anger wanted to rise once more.

"Why?" Killian didn't truly know what he was asking as he released the buffalo demon and stood. Why kill her? Why have Rožė pretend to be his wife? Why do any of this? Even though it wasn't Clove, his body still trembled as if it were—he couldn't unsee her with a dagger in her chest.

"The last of your tasks was to show true anger, and now they are complete." The demon king clapped his hands. "Do you wish to go home?" A grin spread across his face. "Or you can stay here."

Killian wanted to tell Nuodėmė to leave him the hell alone. "Send me home." *Send me home to my family so this can all be a nightmare.*

Nuodėmė gestured for Killian to follow him back to the room with the mirror leading to Clove. Once inside, the demon king produced a handheld mirror from behind his back. At the top of the object rested two horns, and the bottom looked like twisted rope. Same as the dagger before, the entirety of the object was mirror glass, the light above reflecting off its surface.

"Take it," the demon king instructed.

Killian took the object from Nuodėmė's hands and tightened his grip on its cool handle. "What do I do with it?"

"Break it as you did before, and you will go home."

"And Clove?"

"She will live." He placed a hand on Killian's shoulder briefly before stepping back. "Now break the mirror to go home."

Please be true. Lifting the mirror, Killian slammed it against the wall, where it shattered, the sound of breaking glass reverberating as the shards struck the floor.

Killian looked around the room, but he wasn't back at home. He was still here in this glass hell. A tightness formed in his chest, knowing he had been tricked. Yet there had always been a chance. Even if he died then, he and Clove would meet each other again in the Heaven she so believed in because he would choose to believe in it too. Unless this was truly his hell.

Another body appeared on the floor in front of him, her chest heaving. A female demon. Satiny white hair fell to her waist against pearlescent scaled skin like Nuodėmė's. She wore a silky ivory gown, and eyes of silver peered up at him. Triangular mirror horns protruded from her forehead, and her lips were the color of crow wings. Her face fell, full of melancholy, and he *knew* that expression.

"Clove," he rasped.

"You returned my daughter to me." Nuodėmė chuckled. "I have been searching for her for thirteen years. She would have died in your world, but now she won't because you saved her. Without you doing the seven tasks, I couldn't have brought her back home."

"What the hell are you talking about?" Killian asked as the room spun, seeming to close in on him. Something in his chest ached, like it was cracking, and he couldn't find the air to make his lungs move.

"Your wife belongs here, with me. As punishment for her abandoning her family to be with you, I give you seven years of bad luck before you die."

"Killian!" Clove screamed, tears flooding her eyes. "Killian!"

He backed up into the wall instead of toward her. As soon as he realized he should have run to her instead, he was no longer in Veidrodis. Threads and blankets and furniture surrounded him—he was back at home in the craft room. Not standing, but lying on the floor inside his body where Clove had left it beside her rocking chair.

Shakily, he rolled over and released a choked sob. Clove's still body sat in the rocking chair, her eyes wide open, the blanket she had been sewing for their baby resting in her lap.

Killian scooped her dead body from the rocker and cradled her close to his chest. Her body was still warm. But she was *gone*. He sobbed into her hair, wanting her to reach out and stroke his face, tell him that everything was okay.

The demon had been inside Clove. Thirteen years she had been missing from Veidrodis. Killian swallowed, thinking, thinking back to their past. That meant she had been inside Clove's body since they were twelve, when they had grown closer. It was the demon who he loved all this time.

He set Clove's body back in the chair. His hands trembled as he rushed toward the antique mirror. "Clove!" he screamed, pounding his fist on the wall.

"Clove! Come back to me. *Please*." But nothing. There was no answer.

Then realization struck him. He had performed seven tasks for Nuodėmė. *Seven*. Seven deadly sins, like in Clove's Bible.

Greed—taking the grapes. Gluttony—eating the grapes. Pride—killing the demon. Envy—removing his eye. Lust—him spilling himself. Sloth—his deep slumber. Wrath—his anger toward the demon.

All this … all of this was somehow a way to bring the demon king's daughter home. Killian continued to beg for someone to answer him, willing to do anything to undo this. But only silence answered his prayers.

Nuodėmė had said Killian would have seven years of bad luck before he died. He should have known from the beginning to never break a mirror, as his mother had always said. Killian had believed his lucky number was seven. But seven was truly the unluckiest of numbers.

One. Two. Three. Four. Five. Six. Seven.

Dobilai sat in her room—the same one her husband had been in—peering out the mirror at Killian, who had sobbed himself to sleep while calling for her. She pressed her hand to the glass, but he would not see or hear her. In seven years, he would die, and for seven years, she would weep.

The door behind her slid open to her father. As soon as Killian's soul had vanished from the room and returned to his body, her father had left her there to mourn.

"You knew I would find you, daughter," he said.

Dobilai had not. She thought he would never find her. With the help of her servant, Rožė, Dobilai had let her twelve-year-old soul slip from Veidrodis and enter another child who had recently passed. After that, she had quickly become friends with a young boy who she fell in love with. Dobilai had always wanted to be a part of the human world—she had never wanted to be here, and now because of the broken horned mirror, her power was gone. Her father had never treated her wrong—she simply had not agreed with him or this world.

"Father—"

"For seven years, you will stay in this room and watch as your husband withers. For seven years, this will remind you that the abomination which grew in your belly—that was killing you—is now gone. Then when the seven years end, you will become my daughter once more."

Dobilai fought back her tears—demons were not meant to cry, but while being a human, she had learned to *feel*. Had learned to *love*. For the past thirteen years, while in Clove's body, she hadn't forgotten what she truly was. Each day, Dobilai had read her Bible to keep the evil at bay. The moment she had heard Killian from the mirror, she had known he was in Veidrodis. But she could not let him discover the truth because she did not want her father to realize she still knew who she was. Dobilai had thought it could save him. She had also known that if Killian did not complete the tasks her father had set for him, he would have been trapped in Veidrodis and died there. And while he would suffer back in the human world, his soul would not be trapped here.

But hers would be. Alone. So, while Killian would

have seven years of bad luck, she would have an eternity.

"You truly believed you saved him, did you not?" Her father harshly lifted her chin. "His soul will go to Hell, your child will be in Heaven, and you will eternally be here in Veidrodis. The three of you separated forever. In seven years, I will see you again, and we will go on as if none of this ever happened."

Her heart stopped. *Hell*? *No. No. No*!

"Father, please," Dobilai begged, hot tears spilling down her cheeks as he walked away from her.

"See you soon, daughter." The door slid shut behind her father, leaving her alone and shaking. Killian wouldn't be rejoined with their child. He would go to a place that she feared the most, full of burning, torturous flames.

Pressing her hand to the mirror, she whispered, "I will always love you, and if you truly knew me, you would hate me."

Dobilai gathered the broken horned mirror and its glass shards, setting them in front of her. Then she sank to her knees and clasped her hands together in prayer. Though her beloved Bible wasn't at her side, she prayed and prayed, begging the humans' god to hear her call.

Thorna

*T*horna remained outside the great oak tree beside the waterfall in the human world and waited, wearing an ivory gown of silk. She realized she must have looked like a mortal bride on her wedding day. But the color for her meant new, the start of something, if Asher so chose. Pyrka had just finished Thorna's last story before she left and he desperately wanted to know about this one, more than the other tales, what happened next, but again, she had kept her lips sealed.

In the distance, a truck's engine hummed and headlights flooded the forest. Thorna smiled as Asher's truck slipped into view and pulled to a stop not too far from where she stood.

Asher opened the door and stepped out of his truck, the wind ruffling his hair. In his hand rested a small black box.

"You came," Thorna breathed, a tinge of doubt still on the tip of her tongue as she spoke. If he didn't like what she was going to show him next, then he wasn't meant for her. "I'm not what you think I am."

"Thorna," Asher murmured, coming to her in four long strides, pressing his warm hand to her cheek. "I know. I had days to think about it already."

"What do you mean?" she gasped, blinking.

A smile spread across his handsome face. "I already know what you are." He paused, his brown eyes meeting hers. "Or, I may not know exactly what you are. But I know you aren't human."

"How?" Had he seen her when he'd been sleeping on the porch? Perhaps peering out the peephole of his door one night?

"My doorbell has a camera, Thorna." His expression turned sheepish. "So I'm able to check things on my phone."

Ah, yes, the mortals and their technology… Her heart froze in her chest, not knowing if this was a blessing or a curse. But he was here. Yet, was he here because he loved her too, or because he wanted to hurt her?

"Each day," Asher continued. "After reading your first story, I watched the video as you left and saw you turn into the most beautiful moth I'd ever seen. I won't lie—I did freak out the first night, but after that, I only wished you would have stayed. I've missed you coming by the store."

Elation flowed through her, but then a dark feeling halted the emotion when she thought about the word *stayed*. He had wished she stayed *there*.

Thorna cradled his cheek. "I would remain here, I would choose you, but I can't leave my home, my kingdom, my beasties. If I wasn't a queen to my world, I would stay. Perhaps it was selfish of me to think you would leave yours."

"A queen?" he rasped, his throat bobbing.

Taking a deep breath, she nodded. "I'm immortal, a dark fae. If you came with me, you could become immortal, and if I stayed here, I could become human. Or you can walk away if you wish. I'm leaving this story, this tale's ending, up to you." She thought about Pyrka's words, telling her to drag Asher back to her home. Even though a part of her would always itch to if he denied her, she would never force him.

"Your stories," Asher whispered, inching closer to her. "I understood them. Though you may not have meant them to be happy, I know in the future they all were. For tonight, I will start with *Lullaby of Flames*—I'm going to believe Rigel came back from Heaven as an angel to save Cori. Tomorrow, I'll tell you my theory of *Inside the Box*, then the following night another and so on."

This was more than Thorna could have asked for. Asher didn't only read her tales—he wanted to say what he thought about them. Tears pricked her eyes as he handed her the black box. If this was like her stories, Asher may have tried to kill her in that moment, yet he had given her a gift instead.

Chest heaving, Thorna opened the lid, her hand cupping her mouth as she stared at the teacup inside. An emerald moth was printed across the obsidian teacup, her name written beneath in thorned limbs. She set the present beside her on the ground, then threw her arms around his neck, pressing her mouth to his. Thorna's lips molded to Asher's, and they glided across, his movements fueling hers. It was gentle caresses, then demanding sweeps of their tongues. He hoisted her up, her legs circling his narrow hips.

"What now?" Thorna asked, pulling back from his beautiful lips.

"We can start by you showing me your home." Asher leaned close and murmured in her ear, "I choose you."

She arched a brow. "Even my dark side?"

"Every side of you." He grinned.

"The butterflies have been waiting to meet you." Thorna lowered her feet to the ground, grasped his hand,

and pulled him through the barrier to her world.

176

Thorna

Thorna peered at her naked lover, studying his lithe form as he slept. She finished penning two more tales for Asher and placed them at his bedside for when he awoke. Bliss and happiness still coursed through her, and she wanted him again, yet she chose not to disturb him. Another round of lovemaking would come soon enough.

For now, the butterflies required her attention.

Blood Risen

*T*he ground was hard as an icy hell when Hazel slammed the shovel against it, pins and needles shooting up her arms.

"Just let me help," Gray said, leaving his watching post and making a grab for it.

"No, you're not supposed to." Hazel blew out a breath, avoiding Gray's piercing gaze. If he helped her, they would both be punished.

Eight long years Hazel had spent in this nightmare. Most days, it felt like a hundred. Sometimes—incredibly—it felt like home. Because of Gray.

Hazel had been only eleven years old that horrifying day in Tennessee eight years ago. The day she was taken. It had been a beautiful spring day, the purple pansies in full bloom on her walk to school. Her parents had warned her never to talk to strangers, yet the lady wearing green in the driver's seat of a muddy van had been so pretty, seemed so kind. But then, something in her eyes had been all wrong when she held out a piece of fruit, and Hazel knew to run. She hadn't run fast enough. Maybe if she'd run straight to the school instead of the park, they wouldn't have found her hiding behind a boulder. She could still feel its moss-covered surface pressed against her back in her dreams.

Gray had been there too, easily finding her, as if he'd known that was where she would go. "Hide over here," he'd said, pointing toward a large tree trunk. But Hazel hadn't listened and took off toward the closed-in slide of the playground instead.

"My son, Slate, already likes you very much. One day you'll be his chosen wife," the woman, who she later found out to be Gray's mother, had cooed in her ear after discovering her. Then she had pressed something over Hazel's nose and mouth, knocking her out. Later, she'd awoken inside the village with no recollection of how she'd gotten there.

Even when she was locked in the dark, Hazel had believed her parents would come and save her. That her brother and sister would find a way to bring her back home and they would all laugh at her carelessness and have ice cream.

But no one ever came.

And those who did stumble upon this forgotten land met an even worse fate than hers.

"Why is the ground harder this time?" Hazel asked, wiping a hand across the perspiration dotting her brow.

"Because the earth knows a sacrifice is coming soon, and it believes Crolento's gifts to be unnatural, it will fight against it," Gray answered.

"So the sacred text says." Hazel paused, her gaze locking with his. "Do you think things would be different between us if we'd met outside this place?" Each night before she slept, Hazel thought about the bond between them. Would they have even talked? Maybe she would've had the courage to ask him to see a movie in her high school years. High school… She'd never even gotten to finish elementary.

"Everything would've been different," he whispered.

With the word *everything*, she didn't know if it was

good or bad, and she wasn't sure she wanted to know. "What made you decide to talk to me?" When he did, she hadn't trusted him, just as she hadn't his family, or the other villagers. Soon, she hadn't cared. She just needed a friend.

Then she'd needed more.

Gray shrugged and pushed a lock of black hair behind his ear. "Maybe I needed to repent for my sins."

Hazel frowned at his words, her lips parting to reply when footsteps sounded. Gray didn't hesitate to create more space between them.

"Well, there she is," Slate purred, breaking through the branches. "My wife to be." He appeared just as kempt as always, his cotton pants hanging loose, his ivory shirt buttoned to the collar, whereas Gray always left two unfastened.

"The holes aren't coming as fast as I'd like," Hazel said, straightening her spine. "The ground is harder than usual."

"Come on, Gray." Slate combed a hand through his unruly dark hair, then waved his brother on. "Cyan will look after her. We need to prepare for the celebration tonight. It seems Mother may decide to give you a wife soon."

Hazel's heart slammed against her chest. Another celebration. Another. Another. *Another.* Not that many. *One* more. And still, she was dreading it because of what Gray would have to do.

In one week, Hazel was to marry Slate, and if she refused, she would either be forced to or killed. The sacred texts demanded each generation, the first born of the village leader be presented with a pure marital partner on their twenty-first birthday. There were times in her younger years when she'd questioned this place, had wondered if she was meant to be a part of this society. But at night, she'd never stopped her prayers, regardless if her God was real or not.

The sacrifices during the celebration would rouse the creature of the forest—Crolento—to use his seed and flourish their land. On the third celebration night was when she and Gray would escape.

No one alive today had ever seen Crolento, yet when the fruit of the trees shriveled, when the crops withered, the blood spilled onto the land had been enough to feed him and bring life back to full bloom.

It was said in the village's sacred Children of Blood book that if Crolento did choose to rise, he would rip the heart, tongue, and eyes from his sacrifices. Then he would eat the tongue, leaving the villagers to bury the heart and eyes in the earth with a promise that the land would never go barren again. That was why they dug holes before each celebration—in hopes to bury the gifts given by Crolento.

Hazel had witnessed the strangeness of the village, had danced in celebration to what would be considered a miracle to outsiders, but even though she'd never seen Crolento, she believed something was out there. Somewhere.

Tonight, Gray mouthed before turning around. Biting the inside of her cheek, Hazel slammed the shovel back into the earth, this time cracking the surface.

The village women and men were already lining up,

eager to give themselves in celebration of Crolento's gifts. It was believed that pleasure and sacrifice would rouse Crolento, that he fed off the blood and the euphoric emotions.

The love of Hazel's life had already buried himself into another. Both their slick naked bodies glistened with sweat as the fire burned higher, brighter, hotter. Hazel averted her gaze, tried not to clench her jaw as her blood raged inside her veins, spiking a light to her heart that would ignite and explode at any moment. A woman with brown hair mounted Hazel's husband to be, but she didn't give a thorn about Slate.

The village leader, Gray and Slate's mother, Amber, held her blood-red book close to her face, poring over the sacred text. The Children of Blood tome had been handed down for generations and was believed to have come from Crolento.

A wool crimson cloak concealed Amber's body and her dark braid was tucked inside the fabric. She continued to read the scripture—words Hazel had grown used to over the years—while her husband, Hunter, chanted beside her. "Oh, divine Crolento. Take our pleasure. Take our blood. Rise for us this day."

Sometimes Amber and Hunter would finish off the sacrificial celebration coupling with one another alongside the other villagers, but on this cool evening, they remained clothed. Everything of this night was to please the hidden creature of the forest, lure him to their dying crops.

As Gray groaned in pleasure, Hazel did clench her fists then. After her marriage to Slate, she would find herself in this position—her "virginal" blood was to be spilled in front of the village, to feed Crolento. When she'd reached the pleasuring age of sixteen, she'd been relieved she was able to prolong performing. For Gray, if he'd denied his *duty*, his parents would've killed innocent after innocent in front of him until he gave in. Crolento needed to be pleased.

Even if she hadn't fallen in love with Gray, she would've given herself to anyone else to make sure that gift wouldn't have been for Slate.

Amber removed her blade from her cloak pocket while continuing to pour out words from her sacred book. She sliced a thin line across everyone's palm, and Hazel sucked in a sharp breath when her turn came, even though she should be used to the sting by now. Hazel watched the blood spill from her flesh, and the ground below drank it in as though it thirsted for it more than water.

Rusty—an older man Hazel had seen from a distance, tending the fields as he sang hymns—stepped forward and took the blade from Amber. "To feed Crolento all my blood," he said. With a wide smile, Rusty drew a matching one across his throat. He then threw himself into the fire while blood oozed down his throat. Even as the flames licked away his flesh, Rusty didn't scream, and his smile remained. Death, so many deaths since she'd been here, and she hated that she'd grown acclimated to experiencing such gruesome sights.

The ceremony continued, and Hazel stared up at the stars filling the sky, wondering if her family thought about her each night, if they missed her. Or had thoughts of her spread further and further apart over the years, until the last threads of the memory of her split apart?

Mauve, a slender middle-aged woman, escorted Hazel to her small cabin and locked her in as they did every night until she was needed the next day. There wasn't a single window to filter light into her tiny space, leaving Hazel in darkness. She had never been provided much in her cabin, only a place to sleep, red wool dresses folded inside a wicker basket in a corner, and a desk which she hadn't used except to sit and think.

Sinking onto her straw mattress, she drew her knees to her chest like she had when she first arrived to the village. No longer did she feel nineteen, but instead, it was as though she was eleven years old once again.

After a while of counting stars inside her head, the door to her cabin unlocked. Hazel glanced up to find a shadowy form standing in the doorway. The door shut gently and a lantern illuminated the space. Water beaded the ends of Gray's hair, a few of his locks sticking to his chin.

"I'm sorry." Tears slid down Gray's cheeks, yet he didn't step toward her. It wasn't his fault. But whose fault was it? Most of the villagers were born here, grew up with this. There had been others like her, taken. They'd all easily conformed to this, willingly sacrificed themselves to this creature.

With a soft smile, Hazel wrapped her arms around him and he circled his around her, holding her even tighter. For the past seven months, their secret friendship had become something else, and he'd been sneaking into her cabin ever since she'd given him a kiss in the forest. Their kisses had grown bolder, their touches more daring, not an inch of their bodies had been left unexplored by one another.

Gray was only to watch over her. He was meant to one day be for another, but he was Hazel's. Amber had discussed finding him a woman outside the mountains, but there was a widow ten years his senior that his mother had mentioned would be suitable. Numbers had to be kept up—Crolento must be fed.

Hazel inhaled Gray's piney scent, catching a whiff of soap. He'd bathed himself after... She shook off the thought, tucked away the jealousy. "I don't know if I can bear the next few days," she murmured.

"We need to be careful."

Gray was right. She sighed, nodding in agreement. For two days, she would need to distance herself from him. But as she watched the shadows of the lantern dance across the planes of his face, his plump lips, two days seemed an eternity. Hazel brushed a fallen lock behind his ear and cradled his face, capturing his soft mouth with hers. He didn't hesitate, parting his lips, his tongue sweet as honey.

The kiss deepened and Hazel needed him desperately, even though she knew it was a dangerous game they were both playing. But there were no windows, no one to see in, and they would stay quiet as always. Once her body was given to Slate, she was meant to learn the sacred book from him, just as his father had learned from his mother. Gray may have been born here, same as Slate was, but he wasn't like the others who took pleasure in kidnapping and sacrifice. He was too good— he had a conscience and valued human life while no one else seemed to. It was Gray who had planned their escape. Hazel had been locked up for so long that she stopped dreaming of freedom, hadn't known if she would fit back in with the outside. But with his belief in her, *them*, the future, she had forgotten her pain and fear.

"Don't leave yet," she whispered, nipping at his lower lip before loosening the buttons of his shirt and peeling it from his hard body.

"I have a little time." He smiled against her mouth. "Our future together will come soon."

With deft fingers, he drew her wool dress over her head, leaving her bare before him. He bent down, placing a soft kiss between her breasts, to the center of her stomach, before finding her lips once more. Grinning, she unfastened his pants and Gray kicked them away. He groaned as she grasped his hardened length, his mouth slanting over hers, devouring all that was holy inside her.

Gray and Hazel.

Hazel and Gray.

It was never meant to be.

But she repeated their names over and over in her head as she touched, as he explored, as she wanted so much more of him. It didn't matter that he'd been with another at the celebration because he hadn't kissed her like this, touched her like that—it was a duty she knew he did to protect her. Every month this had happened to him over the last four years, and like tonight, her heart had always felt something. The world would claim their love was unholy, that it was because she was captured and taken to an unknown village, but it wasn't. This was something pure, more than light in the darkness. It was hazel in the gray.

"I should leave," Gray said, his breath raspy in her ear as he gently lay her on the mattress. "But I don't want to."

"I don't want you to either." She trailed her hands up his back, her fingers entangling in his damp hair.

He pushed inside her and her back arched as she gasped in pleasure. Since their first kiss, their bodies had grown to claim one another, discovered more about the other. His dips, his scars, his desires.

The goats bleated outside, as they always did, and Hazel released a small snort. Gray chuckled into the crook of her neck until their laughter subsided and the urge to drive one another to bliss, to escape, took control. She muffled her cries as euphoria exploded along her every cell, then captured his mouth in a kiss while he groaned, letting his seed fill her.

Gray rolled her over, holding her close. "Forget waiting a couple of days. I don't want to risk you being here anymore."

Fear nagged at her, warning her against the risk not to go, but maybe tonight was better, since the celebrations had begun and most would still be drunk on wine.

"We won't take anything," Gray said, throwing on his clothing. "You're all I need."

She slipped her simple dress over her head and drew on her torn slippers. There was nothing Hazel owned in this hell anyway. When she was stolen, all she'd had was a backpack full of books and her clover locket from her parents. Her necklace had been taken by Amber and thrown into the fire at one of the celebrations long ago.

Gray slowly opened the door, glancing both ways before nodding and grasping her hand. He tugged her through the door, and as the wind rumpled her hair, it seemed to promise freedom.

The fire had died down and only the ashes remained, cloaking the pair in darkness. However, the moon cast its silvery glow down on the circular rows of cabins. Nothing besides the sounds of insects' buzzing filled the night air.

Holding a finger over his lips, Gray pointed across the village toward the lush forests and mountains beyond.

They hurried in that direction, their steps silent, until a sickening crack struck her eardrum. Something wet covered Hazel's face, and she jerked to a stop.

"What was that?" Hazel hissed, turning to face Gray, only he didn't look back at her. She still held his hand as his headless corpse fell to the earth. She blinked. Blinked again.

She didn't release Gray's hand as she gazed at his headless body near his decapitated head. His eyes stared blankly up at her while her chest heaved. Horror rocketed through her and she was unable to look away, unable to *believe*.

He was… He was dead.

Two strong arms encircled her then, squeezing and yanking her to a strong chest. "Look at the mess you've caused." Slate's deep voice boomed in her ear, a bloody axe resting in his hand.

"I should've known you'd be trouble the day Gray chose you to come here," Hunter rasped, stepping in front of them with disheveled hair.

Gray had picked her. *Gray*. As dread washed over her, the liquid dripping down her cheek burned. Gray's blood.

Hazel screamed then, heavy and shrill, the sound of terror. The sound she hadn't made since she had first been brought to the village all those years ago.

The floorboards creaked as Hazel paced. She was back in her home, which wasn't really a home at all. Even now as she thought about her real home in Tennessee, she could only remember bits and pieces as though it had all been a dream. A wonderful dream until she'd woken to this nightmare.

For the rest of the night and day, Hazel had been unable to sleep because she knew they were going to find out… Since she'd met Gray, she had always believed he wasn't meant to be here. But he'd been the one to pick her out, pluck her like a piece of fruit from a tree.

Hot tears rained down her cheeks as Hazel sobbed through the sounds of the second night's celebration. Even though anger penetrated her grief, she still loved Gray. She couldn't blame him though—he had been only a child, same as her. However, it was her fault he was dead. They should've waited the two days like they had originally planned.

Even with plots of escape when she first arrived, Hazel had become too frightened because she could barely swim, let alone survive to find her way out. As the years passed, the hopeless situation felt more and more as though it were too late for freedom. But as she learned from Gray, it was never too late.

An inhuman shriek filled the forest, the sound at once terrifying and heartbreaking. Hazel froze inside her cabin. It was a sound she'd never heard before. Not a bear, nothing of that sort. She rushed to the wall and pressed her ear up against it, listening. Another guttural wail came, chilling her to the bone. Hazel thought about the village's sacred texts. Crolento was said to maintain their crops and fruit from the earth. But all she could think about were the demons of the Bible when she would go to Sunday school with her parents. Her hands trembled and her breaths stayed lodged in her throat—if a demon were to make a sound, this would be it.

"Hazel," a deep voice whispered.

Heart pounding violently in her chest, she spun at what she knew to be Gray's voice. But he wasn't there. She expected him to walk through the door as he always did, yet he couldn't—seeing his slain body was proof of that. The door unlocked, then creaked open, and her lips parted, her chest tightening.

Slate stood beside his father, both wearing crimson cloaks, their eyes narrowed. "Crolento has chosen to rise and come for you after you destroyed Gray and deceived me with your sins," Slate spat.

"You're delusional, you—" Hazel's words trailed off as something not of this world passed through the open door. *Crolento…* The skeletal creature towered above them, his massive curved horns brushing the ceiling, his spine curved. Hairless flesh, the color of dried blood, hung loose from his bones as if he had starved for years. His face was eyeless, his nose long and pointed. As Crolento's dark lips parted, rows of sharp teeth gleamed in the lantern's light. He sniffed at the air, a deep rumble spilling from his mouth.

Crolento drew closer, and she backed up to the other wall. A pleasant scent coming from the creature, like pine, *familiar*, brushed her senses. There was nowhere else to go and the door was blocked by Slate and Hunter. The floorboards groaned beneath Crolento and his fingers grasped her shoulder. A squeak escaped her, and she was too stricken to do anything else as claws protruded.

"Stop," she murmured. "Please."

Crolento leaned in, his nose brushing hers, *inhaling*. He crouched in front of her stomach, and Hazel's eyes widened in horror as he sniffed the area. Her gaze darted to Hunter and Slate, but it was too late. She knew they could see the slight bulge of her stomach. Crolento sniffed once more and his hand released her before turning away. Slate and Hunter sank to their knees, bowing as the creature passed them.

For the first time in his life, Slate looked like he couldn't breathe while he gripped the front of his shirt. "Do we sacrifice her ourselves?"

"She's with child," Hunter growled, taking Hazel by the arm and digging his fingers into her skin.

Hazel clenched her teeth—she'd known a baby was growing inside her for at least four months now. Gray had known. That was the true reason that finally drove them to risk their lives to escape.

"After the babe comes, we'll call Crolento to return for her," Hunter seethed. "We'll make sure of it. You could've had a wonderful life here with Slate. Instead, you and Gray both proved to be whores. You'll be dead like my son soon enough."

Fear shot through Hazel—this was worse, so much worse. After the failed escape, she'd meant to die by their hands, to take her baby with her to the grave, but now, her child would become *theirs*. And she didn't know what the village would twist him or her into.

"I suppose I'll have to claim another." Slate shrugged.

"I curse you!" Hazel spat, anger rocketing through her, boiling her blood. "Crolento will find you and tear you apart limb by limb for your sins."

Slate released a deep rumble of laughter. "You have no power. You're no one."

As the door slammed shut, she imagined her own screams filling the air, her eyes getting ripped out, her tongue being plucked, and then, finally, her heart leaving its rib cage. This creature was *real*, and she'd seen him with her own eyes. He had *touched* her.

Clutching her stomach, she dropped to the floor and pressed her head against the wall. She cried then, let out every sorrow she held. They knew… They knew… And they would take her baby once it was born.

Hazel closed her eyes and prayed as her mother had taught her. But this time, she didn't pray to her God. Instead, she prayed to Crolento. Prayed he would tear into Slate and Hunter before he left. Prayed he would destroy the village to keep new people from being brought here. When she opened her lids, a shadow crept across the room toward her, and she gasped as the figure became clearer. *Gray.*

"You kept a secret from me," she whispered. "You picked me for your brother." The bit of anger that had been with her earlier vanished and she rushed forward to wrap her arms around him. But they passed through, a coldness prickling her skin.

Her eyes widened when she slowly slid her hand through him once more to prove he indeed wasn't whole. A ghost…

"I know. I should've told you, and I was going to." He sighed, appearing the same as he had on the night he'd died. There wasn't a single line marring his neck where the axe had sliced clean through. "But I was still a child then, stupid, foolish, and not truly knowing anything but this village. Yet when I saw you, you were like a breath of fresh sunshine and I only wanted to be around you. Even then, I tried to get you to hide in a different spot, remember?"

Hazel nodded. "Are you really here? A spirit? Or am

I imagining this?"

Gray bit his lip and reached for her hand—it still wouldn't connect. "I am, but not for long. I need to confess something else to you."

A chill crawled up her spine—what else could there be to confess that was worse than this predicament? "What is it?"

"You met Crolento tonight, yes?" Gray drew the words out slowly.

"He rose." Hazel's hands trembled. "Just tell me what it is, Gray. I know when you're about to tell me something I won't like."

"When my brother murdered me, my soul became one with Crolento. He hadn't risen in centuries, only our blood feeding him through the land, but that blood created something, something dark that needed to come from a cruel family death, not a sacrifice. I escaped Crolento this once, yet I don't think I'll be able to again. Because I am him."

Hazel sucked in a sharp breath, refusing to believe it. But then she remembered the familiar pine smell of Crolento … it was Gray. "And I don't suppose you can open the door in this form to let me help you?"

Gray shook his head, raking a hand through his dark hair. "I can't, but when I'm torn from here and placed back inside Crolento, I'll fight with everything in me to."

"After the baby is born, they're going to sacrifice me to you." She paused, pursing her lips. "For you to eat."

"Inside the creature, I liked the way you smelled, but everything is fading." Gray groaned, gripping the side of his skull.

"Don't go," Hazel begged, her voice unsteady as her hand slipped through his form once more.

And then Gray was ripped away from her, vanishing through the wall, back within Crolento.

Day after day, month after month, Hazel sat in her room, except for when she was allowed out to tend to the crops and livestock, even as her belly grew larger and she became more exhausted. Not once had Gray returned over the past four and a half months, and she hadn't expected him to. Although she had wished it.

Crolento hadn't returned either. Yet villagers continued to sacrifice themselves monthly in Crolento's name, cutting out their own tongues and eyes, as if it was a blessing to do these things.

But now the day she dreaded was here. Another sharp pain spread across her back and Hazel doubled over. She wouldn't have had much experience with childbirth if she lived back home, but she'd helped deliver several babies throughout the years in the village.

Shoving a rag between her teeth and hiking up her dress, she settled on top of her mattress as sweat dripped down her neck. Another stab to the back came, ripping across her stomach. Hazel's eyelids fluttered, but she wouldn't cry for help—she would not alert anyone the baby was coming. No one would have the child except for her.

A warm liquid pooled around her thighs and she fought against the pains slicing through her. More and more strikes of agony stormed inside her stomach. Harder and harder she bit down on the cloth until there was an instinctual need within her to push. *Breathe. Push.*

Breathe. Push. Once the baby's head was visible, she reached between her legs and guided it out.

But babies didn't understand the need to keep silent. They didn't understand danger. And so Hazel's daughter did what every baby did upon entering the world—she cried.

"No," Hazel whispered between gritted teeth. Then using a ragged dress as a blanket, she wrapped it around the child to prepare to flee. But when the door flew open to Mauve and her two sons, Hazel was too weak and stumbled as she tried to dart around them.

The taller son yanked her back, while Mauve tore the baby from Hazel's arms. The younger son shoved Hazel to the floor and they slammed the door, locking it behind them. Sobbing, Hazel sat alone bleeding on the floor, and she didn't have the strength to even change out of her dress. No one brought in fruit or even a glass of water.

She didn't know how much time had passed when the door finally opened and Slate walked in. His lip curled in disgust as he looked from her bed to where she was huddled on the floor. There were no weapons for her to wield, not even a fork. All her food had always been brought in without any silverware so she had to eat with her hands like a prisoner.

"Ivory will be raised as my daughter and will know me as her father. You will have never existed." Slate barreled forward, and it didn't take much for him to tie her arms behind her back and her ankles together from her pathetic weakness.

"Thanks to you," he continued, "I have a wife who pleases me in every way I see fit. She will bear me children, but for now, Ivory is the perfect gift for her."

Hazel somehow drew the strength to spit a pitiful

amount of saliva on his boot, but it was enough to make the edges of her lips tilt up.

"Cunt," Slate growled. He hoisted her over his shoulder, her gaze studying his back, and her stomach lurched. If she'd had any food in there, she would've expelled it all.

Moments later, Slate tossed her to the ground inside the forest. "There, see if you can escape now."

Curling to her side after he left, Hazel tried to wriggle across the ground, but it did no good. She wasn't even attempting to distance herself from the village but return to it. For her daughter. Chest heaving, she propped herself against a tree. She drew the rope under and over her legs so her hands dangled in front of her.

Beside her rested plenty of rocks and she snatched the sharpest one she could find to saw at the ropes. Every time she swallowed, it was like sandpaper and she desperately needed a drink, but she continued to cut. And then, through the pregnant silence of the landscape, the loud wail of a creature shot through the air, shrill then deep. Hazel shuddered but scolded herself—she wouldn't be afraid. It was Gray. Somewhere buried in Crolento was the man she loved.

Out from the darkness, the hulking form came, his shadow crawling toward her. The creature stopped, his chest moving in sync with the sounds of the wind as he knelt before her. Gray's elongated fingers lifted her greasy hair and inhaled. Sharp teeth bared, he drifted to her stomach, sniffing her. A low growl vibrated from his lips that she could feel down to her bones. She held her breath, preparing for him to rip pieces from her, to *eat* her. But when he growled again at her stomach, she knew it was for something else.

"Gray," she murmured, placing a hand against his horn. "Gray, please, help our daughter. I'm too weak. You don't want her to become a monster like the others. You aren't a monster. They are."

His breath hitched and even without eyes, he seemed to meet her gaze. And she didn't see him as Crolento, a creature, only her Gray.

He placed a warm hand on her forehead—a soothing sensation flowed through her, returning her strength, just as the crops and fruit had become healthy after past sacrifices. She held out her arms, and he sliced both her bindings with his sharp claws.

Without waiting for her, Gray hobbled toward the village, and she grabbed the sharp rock before catching up with him. If he hadn't healed her in what she could only describe as magic or witchery, then she wouldn't have been able to stand.

Darkness had already fallen and everyone was locked away in their cabins for the night. Silently, they approached Slate's logged home, where the wind clanked the metal chimes. Gray thrust a foot forward, breaking the door's lock and blowing it wide open.

Slate stormed into the sitting room, naked with his new wife—Azure—bare beside him. Gray didn't hesitate as he leapt forward, his massive claws grasping Slate's head, tearing it from his shoulders. Blood sprayed the walls, and Slate's body slumped to the floor, the way Gray's had all those months ago. Azure moved toward them, but Hazel slammed her fist into the woman's jaw, knocking her to the ground, unconscious. Hazel shook out her hand, the bones throbbing, but she ignored the pain as she searched the room for her daughter, only to find she wasn't there.

Panic coursed through her, but there was one place she was certain where the infant would be. "The baby will be at your parent's house," Hazel said while grabbing a knife from beneath the bed and sprinting out the door toward Amber and Hunter's home, a short jog away.

Her lungs were like concrete in her chest when she stopped in front of their door. She couldn't kick it open the way Gray had and wouldn't risk it either. Giving him a brief nod, she stepped back and allowed him to strike the door with his heel, like lightning shattering the village.

No one was in the sitting room, only their wooden chairs and the sewing table, where Amber would make her cloaks. In the corner of the bedroom, cowering on the floor, was Hunter and Amber, the baby resting in her hands.

"Give me my daughter," Hazel demanded, taking a step forward, not showing an ounce of fear, no matter how hard her heart beat.

"I'll break her neck if you step closer," Amber said, her nostrils flaring.

"And then you'll die anyway." Hazel wouldn't cower, not when she'd lived in fear for eight years. "If you want to stay alive, put my daughter on the mattress."

Amber didn't budge. But as Gray took a heavy step forward, Amber paled and set the baby on the mattress, then slowly backed into the corner, bowing her head.

"I didn't say how long you would live though. Make it hurt, Gray," Hazel said in a low voice.

As he tore toward the corner, Hazel smiled, ignoring the pained screams, while she lifted her daughter in her arms. The infant's eyes were still closed, her breaths soft.

Dark patches of hair, the color of Gray's, sat along her tiny scalp. "You don't look like an Ivory, you look like an Izzy."

After Gray's parents were nothing but torn flesh and bone, Hazel swayed, exhaustion washing over her. Gray scooped her and Izzy into his arms, holding them close, and the heavy scent of blood caressed her nose. Finally, she rested in his arms as he carried her and their daughter through the night, through the emerald forest and over the mountains until they reached the place where the edge of trees met a road.

Gray lowered Hazel to her feet, and they studied one another for a long while. The dark eyes she always stared into weren't there, but she felt as though he could see all of her in that moment. His hand lifted, a hair's breadth from brushing her cheek, when two bright lights shone through the darkness. Hazel whirled around, her gaze focusing on … something. It took her a moment to recognize what it was, what she was seeing. Headlights from a car.

With a relieved smile, she turned back to Gray, but he was already gone.

When the village was searched, it was found to be deserted. Hazel was uncertain if the villagers had all simply left, or if Gray had slaughtered them. Deep down, she believed the second to be true.

After six months of being free, rumors had spread of a creature deep in the forest of the mountains whose wails haunted any who heard them. It was believed the creature cried for its lost love.

At night, Hazel would cry out too.

Her daughter cried out, interrupting Hazel's thoughts.

"It's okay, Izzy. We're going somewhere special," Hazel said as she unbuckled her daughter's car seat. They'd driven a while to reach this secluded area, and one day she would return forever, but for now, she needed to raise her daughter where she would thrive the most.

Hazel lifted Izzy onto her hip and entered the lush forest. The scent of pine enveloped her, becoming stronger the farther she walked. Dry leaves crunched and she jerked her chin up to find a deep red form with curving horns slipping out from behind a gnarled tree.

Gray.

Hazel's heart swelled at the sight of him, no matter that he didn't look like the boy he'd once been. It was still him. A smile spread across her face as she stepped toward her love. "Your daughter and I missed you."

Sweet as Honey

The palest of snowflakes drifted from the night sky as though the stars were shedding layers of themselves to gather along the forest floor. Hansel pushed back a lock of blond hair from his face and held his lantern higher. His arm ached as he peered into the gloom, and his feet were frozen solid, but he trudged on, determined to find his sister.

Gretel should have arrived a week ago, and that she had not was unthinkable. She was a person of her word, never late, not once in her life. Hansel had no choice but to search for his sister. Gretel would have sent word if she had been retained, knowing how protective her brother was of her. Knowing he would worry himself sick, refuse to rest, make himself ready and willing to brave any forest in search of her the moment he even suspected she had met trouble.

Ever since they were children, the siblings had been close. After their mother succumbed to the plague that invaded her young body, they'd been gifted an oblivious father who drank all the time and a stepmother who beat them with anything she could find. A stepmother who'd been too cowardly to kill her stepchildren with her own vile hands, content to let the forest do her dirty work for her.

Hansel took a deep breath of the crisp air, remembering those younger days when Gretel would stash pebbles in her raggedy dress pockets, or Hansel would carry marbles in his torn trousers. They'd always found their way back home until their stepmother took away their pebbles and marbles. They had used meager breadcrumbs next, seeing as that was all they'd had left. Yet the crows had eaten the crumbs up, and the siblings had never found their way home again. They might have starved, if not for the kind woodcutter who took them in after he discovered them lost and hungry, willing to take shelter in an old cottage, its roof hardly a roof at all, resting in the middle of the woods.

Hansel stared up at the moon and took another swig of whiskey, letting the lantern guide him through the trees. As the alcohol burned his throat, he knew he was becoming his father. A drunkard. While Gretel worked for a wealthy family and their two children to better herself. The man of the home was unkind to his children which was why she stayed, to show the little ones love, regardless that he treated Gretel the same way. If the man had roughed her up, Hansel swore on his life he would kill him, shred him to pieces.

His stomach knotted at the thought of something truly horrific happening to her. She was all he had left after the woodcutter passed away last winter. And now Hansel was twenty-four, no longer a boy, and could take care of himself. He should be able to do the same for Gretel.

As Hansel trekked on through the snow, his body ached, growing weaker, and his throat became dry like sandpaper. He guzzled down his whiskey until there wasn't a drop left. The forest spun around him and the wind blew harder, the chill passing through his flesh and straight to his bones. If he still had a horse, he would have brought the animal with him, but he'd given the mare to Gretel in case she needed to escape her current situation.

Perhaps that was what had happened… But no, she would have contacted him somehow.

His sister swore she would never settle down with a family, but she wanted Hansel to. With each recent visit, she asked when he would take a wife and have children so she could fatten them up with sweets.

One day, he would tell her even though he wasn't certain he wanted that for himself. Perhaps he was meant to be alone, making weapons in his shop. His heart still ached from the time he'd fallen in love with someone—Katrin—but she had thrown him aside in favor of another. The only company he chose to have since then were the prostitutes at the brothel when he needed to find release. Sometimes two, sometimes three at a time. One riding his length, another his face, while his hand stroked a female's mound. A wicked desire, a blissful distraction.

The snow sloshed beneath Hansel's boots and at that moment he wished he was at a brothel, a warm body mounted on top of him instead of trekking around in the cold, like a fool.

Howls echoed through the trees, too near for his liking. Wolves. His rifle rested at his back, and he fished it out, but his feet stumbled before he could steady it. A sickness swam through his blood, weakening him further, more than the effects of alcohol. He needed to take a break, find rest.

Just ahead, a small cottage caught his attention—the same one he and Gretel had almost gone to years ago. There'd been a rumor back then that a witch lived in the cottage, and a few years later her body was found, bloody and dismembered. It was said someone in the town had sought revenge for their missing child.

Each visit to see Hansel, Gretel would pass the familiar cottage, mentioning how it was still empty.

Stopping for the night at the home that once belonged to a woman who murdered children wouldn't have been his first choice, but Hansel's body could carry him no farther.

As he approached the cottage, it looked nearly the same, only more crooked. Light cracks marred the deep brown wood and patches of the chestnut roof were missing, but the windows were spotless.

Hansel walked up the creaking steps and the door opened. He froze, lifting his rifle. A young woman, beautiful and lithe, with straight obsidian hair cascading to her waist, pale skin, and dark eyes stood there with a lantern and an axe.

She released a small screech and took a step back, lifting her weapon, her black frock hugging her curves. "What are you doing on my porch?"

"I thought this place was empty," Hansel said, lowering his rifle, his body swaying from exhaustion.

"Clearly not." She held the axe higher.

"I'm not feeling well and there are wolves about." As though to prove he wasn't lying, howling reverberated around them.

The woman narrowed her eyes, then sighed. "All right. Go inside and warm yourself by the fireplace. But if you try anything untoward, I'll remove your limbs."

"Thank you for the relief, my name's Hansel. I promise I won't hurt you." He stepped inside, inhaling a mixture of cinnamon and vanilla.

"I'm Mabel." The woman lit candles around the sitting room, all the while watching him carefully. "I'll fetch wood from outside. Remember, if you try anything when I get back—”

“Yes, I know.” He rolled his eyes. “You’ll remove my limbs.”

“Glad we understand one another.” But he could see the twitch of her plump red lips, a mouth that looked to be made for tasting. “Now, let me hurry before the wolves show up. I wouldn’t want to become their dinner because of you luring them here.”

Before he could say a word, Mable was out the door. Hansel set his belongings on the floor beside a fur rug. The room was a decent size with two wooden chairs, a settee stacked with quilts, and a sewing table in the corner. The cottage appeared to be well kept with not a speck of dust as though Mabel had been staying here for a little while at least.

Hansel sank down onto the fur rug in front of the fireplace where only glowing ashes remained. His eyes threatened to close and with each passing moment, his mouth grew drier. The door opened, and Mabel shut it with her boot before carrying the armful of logs to the fireplace. She set them on top of the ashes and took a few moments to coax the flames to life—a bright orange fire crackled with warmth, brightening the room.

“How long have you been staying here?” he asked, his gaze drifting from her sparkling dark eyes to her shapely lips.

“Some time after it was abandoned.” She shrugged.

“You mean after the woman thought to be a witch was murdered?”

“I don’t believe she was a witch. I believe she either got what she deserved, or she didn’t.”

He coughed as sweat trickled down his face and neck.

Before he could speak, she pressed a finger to his mouth, her other hand to his forehead, and continued, "Stop talking. You're only going to make your fever worse. Let me collect some things for you while you remove your clothing. A blanket is on the settee behind you."

His eyelids fluttered at the feel of her delicate finger against his mouth, and Hansel resisted the temptation to flick his tongue along her soft flesh.

As Mabel left the room, a numb sensation began to travel from Hansel's fingertips to his lips and down to his toes. He held his hands up to the fire, but he could barely feel its prickling heat. Perhaps it was the whiskey, yet he'd never been like this after drinking. Even when he'd had bottle after bottle of it.

Hansel drew his tunic over his head, followed by his boots and trousers, setting them beside his rifle and satchel. The blanket was scratchy against his skin, and he covered his lower half before returning to the fur rug.

Mabel's skirts swished as she entered the room, her feet now bare. She held a wet cloth in one hand and a pillow in the other. "Lay down," she instructed.

He did as told, his eyes lingering on her curves briefly. She fluffed up the pillow for him, then she applied the cool cloth to his head, her fingers brushing his temple.

"Let me get you something to drink." Her face softened slightly, and she left the room before returning with a glass of pale-yellow liquid along with a loaf of bread.

"What is that?" He would drink anything in that moment, regardless of the taste.

"Sweet water. Hopefully, something that will get you out of my house soon." The edges of her lips tilted up, and she handed him the cup.

"And if it doesn't?" He managed a small smirk.

She cocked her head. "I suppose we'll have to come up with an alternative."

He drank the cool, velvety liquid down, water sweeter than any he'd ever tasted. Like pure nectar and honey. "It's good."

"My sister showed me its healing properties when we were young."

"I was traveling in search of my sister." He paused, scanning the bare walls. "Why are you staying out here all alone?"

"Perhaps I don't like to be near anyone." Mabel placed a piece of bread into his mouth, and he chewed. It was fluffy and savory, but his tastebuds yearned for more of the sweet liquid.

"Can I have another glass of your water?"

"Too much might make you sicker. I'll give you more in the morning." She took a seat across from him and watched him with a guarded expression, neither of them saying a word. Hansel studied Mabel's heart-shaped face, features some might consider cold, but he could see the delicate beauty beneath. Her shoulders relaxed as though she realized he wasn't going to try and harm her. Not that he would, but he couldn't in his current state anyhow.

Hansel closed his eyes, and the weakness started to fade as a new craving took root when he thought about Mabel's scarlet lips and the figure he wanted to see beneath her fitted dress.

He pushed down the thoughts and tried to sleep, but when a soft hand stroked his face, then those silky pads of her fingertips skimmed down his neck, his chest, his abdomen, to the trail of hair leading beneath the blanket, he couldn't. Hansel's heart beat wildly inside his rib cage, yearning for those fingers to slip underneath the scratchy layer and touch him, for those plump lips to sink down and taste his length. It had been too long since he'd visited the brothel, and for the first time in a while, this woman he just met was someone he might want to learn more of. The way he had with Katrin before she left him.

Hansel wanted this craving to be sated now, not wait months like he had with Katrin. If Mabel wanted to wait, he would, but by the way her fingers were fondling his skin, she needed touching as much as he did. She had to be lonely here without another to bring her to bliss the way he could.

He opened his eyes to a pair of dark irises. Mabel leaned over him, the pale skin of her throat calling to him to be kissed by his lips.

"This may be forward, but I want to touch you," he whispered. "If I do anything you don't like, you're free to remove one of my limbs."

"I like a forward man," Mabel said. "Yet I like a forward woman more." She laughed softly, her inviting gaze locked on his, then she loosened the first button of her dress, proving her boldness, her enticing forwardness. The fabric dropped to the floor into a dark heap, and his eyes became hooded as he drank her in. Her body was perfection, unlike anything he could have dreamt. A body like an hourglass, her breasts exquisitely full with pebbled rosebud nipples. That creamy skin seemed to have barely been licked by the sun was desperate for his tongue.

Hansel pushed the blanket away from him and drew her atop him, her softness hugging his hardness. He needed to suck in a nipple before pressing his lips to hers.

As he did just that, Mabel moaned, arching into him, her hips shifting forward, making his length hard as stone. And then his mouth found hers, his tongue dipping between the seams of her lips, flicking against hers, tasting like the sweetest of pastries. He slanted his lips over Mabel's, devouring her luscious flavor.

Mabel's hands glided over his chest as she kissed her way across his throat. Her tongue circled his nipple then trailed down his chest and stomach. As her tongue then gathered the pearl from his tip and pressed her mouth around his cock, taking him in, the pleasure he felt was better than any he'd experienced at the brothels he'd visited, even better than Katrin.

Hansel weaved his fingers in Mable's feather-soft hair, groaning while she licked, sucked, her hand pumping him with wondrous precision. When he felt he would come, he drew her up to him, kissing those lovely lips of hers before flipping her to her back. He wanted to taste that pretty mouth of hers once more before driving into her.

Hansel's hand drifted between Mable's legs, rubbing as he nibbled at her neck, sucking the flesh beneath her ear. He wanted to mark her, *claim her*, because once he found Gretel to be safe, he would come back and they would bring pleasure to one another again and again.

His mouth fell to her core, and she tasted even sweeter there, so damn sweet like sugar and icing. Hansel plunged his tongue inside her, lapping up her flavor, then swiped it slowly up her center. He didn't want to stop but his cock needed to feel her heat. *Desperately.*

"Turn over," he rasped.

"Hmm," she purred. "Seems I'm trusting you too easily."

"I can stop if you wish?"

"Don't stop unless I say to." Mabel turned to all fours, and Hansel got to his knees, stroking his cock while she peered over her shoulder, her gaze ravenous. In one swift motion, he thrust inside of her, and Hansel relished the elation that filled him when she jerked forward with a delightful gasp. Another moan elicited from her ruby lips as he gently pulled back and slammed inside her once more.

Mabel felt so good, so tight as though she'd never done this before, but he was sure she had with her practiced movements, touches. But he didn't care if she'd been with the entire world because right now it was her and him, and he thrust again. Again and again. Harder, faster. Her breasts bounced, their bodies glistening with sweat. He couldn't get enough of her, and when her core clenched around his length as she came, he cried out, spilling his seed into her.

Hansel closed his eyes, his chest heaving while he hovered atop her. Mable's heart beat through her back and flowed into him. He kneaded her breasts, wanting her to ride his cock next, then ride his mouth.

Not wanting the moment to end, Hansel slowly peeled open his eyes, his body aching.

"Are you all right?" Mabel asked, removing the cloth from his forehead. "You feel hotter. Maybe I should make you another glass of sweet water now."

Hansel took a deep swallow, taking in that Mabel was fully dressed, not naked, not crimson from bliss. It had been a ridiculous lust-filled dream, and he was so damn hard and thankful he had a blanket covering him or else she would see how needful his desire was.

"Thank you," he croaked, the two words a chore to

get out.

Mabel left the room, returning with another glass of sweet water. He drank the cool liquid down, his throat growing less dry by the second. His heart still raced from the images of his dream, and he prayed she couldn't somehow hear it.

As he studied her, thinking about her all alone in the middle of the woods, in this old cottage where a murderer once lived, words he hadn't expected to say escaped his mouth. "If you need a place to stay, I have an extra room."

She arched a brow at him. "We just met, remember?"

"We did, but do you really want to stay in these woods forever? I can help. My weapons shop could use an extra pair of hands." Gretel had worked there, but once their caregiver passed, she couldn't handle the memories any longer.

"Maybe." Mabel smiled softly and wiped the damp hair from his forehead. She placed another cool cloth on his skin. "Get some rest."

But all Hansel could think of as he closed his eyes was how real her body had felt against his, how he wished he could have that dream again.

Hansel awoke to Mabel replacing another cloth on his forehead. He stirred each time she performed the task, but this time he was wide awake. She stared down at him, her lips pursing. "Do you need more sweet water already?"

He needed more than sweet water—he wanted her. Biting his lip, he grasped her wrist, his thumb rubbing her smooth skin gently.

"Fuck me," he whispered. Hansel couldn't contain himself, not with the pleasureful dream earlier, with how sweet Mabel looked, with how pretty she was, how kind to a stranger she'd been, regardless of her sharp tongue at first—he needed her, needed to see if that tongue tasted as sweet as it had in his dream.

"I should regret you coming to my door, but I don't," she murmured.

Hansel grinned as she allowed him to lift her dress over her head. Mabel's body was precisely how it had been in his dream. He couldn't think too much on it because when she sank down on him, a heavenly rush of ecstasy rushed through him. And then she rolled her hips forward, his fingers drifting from her waist to her apple of an ass. He gripped her soft flesh, driving himself deeper into her heat. Pulse pounding, he bucked his hips, meeting her in the loveliest of dances, a rapture of bliss.

Hansel sat up, digging his fingers into her flesh even more, his mouth taking in one of her peaked nipples. The sweetest of flavors, like chocolate and berries, hit his tongue. Mabel tasted just as good as she had in his reverie, her skin like licorice, and he wanted to taste her bundle of nerves but he couldn't stop. Not with how good their bodies were igniting one another's. It was as though her mouth and tongue were unraveling all his layers. A rush of pleasure barreled through him and he closed his eyes, giving all of himself inside her.

He licked his lips with a smile and opened his eyelids, prepared to allow himself a moment so he could take her from behind as he had in his dream. Only, Mabel wasn't on top of him. She was fully dressed, resting in the chair, her head tilted to the side as she slept.

What the hell? He could still feel *everything*.

Hansel needed to go to Gretel, but his body was weak again, not strong like it had been in his dreams when he'd been… He shook off the thought, not wanting Mabel to know what he'd been conjuring in his mind. But as he took in her soft sleeping features, curiosity filled him. He wanted to know more about her.

"Your fever is getting worse." Mabel sighed. She brought Hansel another glass of sweet water along with a sweet paste she pressed onto his tongue. "I'm not sure if this is good enough, but it's all I have. I may need to venture out."

"I'll be fine," he slurred. "Tell me something about you."

"I love the winter, the ice and snow." She smiled, her fingers folding around his. "Even though you're a nuisance, you're keeping me on my toes."

Hansel shrugged, growing bold. "Enough of a nuisance to grant me a kiss?"

Mabel stilled, her lips parting. Hansel wasn't certain what she was going to do, but then she slowly knelt and pressed her mouth to his. It was only briefly but there was a hint of honey from the tea she'd just polished off. "If you get better, I'll give you another."

"I'll gladly wait."

All Hansel could do over the next few days was eat, drink, and sleep. Yet every time he slept, he was at his fullest, healthy—and always, *always*, fucking and tasting Mabel in every position imaginable. When awake he knew he needed to seek out his sister, but he couldn't. Not when he couldn't even bring himself to stand. The sweet water was heavenly when he was awake, and the sex was devilish when he was asleep. It was a twisted oblivion he wanted to remain in forever.

Hansel woke to Mabel tracing his lips with her fingertips. "Sorry I disturbed you," she said.

He sat up, his muscles and joints aching. "I wouldn't mind you doing it again. Perhaps another kiss?"

"Gretel told me about you." She grinned. "Told me how a wench of a woman had ruined her brother."

Hansel's brow furrowed. "How do you know my sister's name?" He hadn't mentioned her name to Mabel, not a single time that he could recollect. Or had he?

She pressed her lips to his, and the sweetness of her mouth distracted him for a moment. When she drew back her eyes were pitch black, darker than any night sky. "Because she tasted just as good as you. When I fucked her in her dreams and when I ate her later."

Hansel's throat bobbed and his breaths grew ragged. "What did you say?"

Onyx leathery wings sprung from Mabel's back, her ears elongating into fine points, and Hansel's eyes widened in horror. He crawled away from her, his back colliding with the wall. What *was* she? This was a dream, another just as before. *Wake up. Wake up.*

"You aren't dreaming this time, Hansel. You never were. It was too easy for you to drink my faerie wine. The woman before me who lived here wasn't a witch—she was innocent, but I happily gave her a death." Her dark irises glistened as she bared razor-sharp teeth.

"You're a witch…" His chest heaved, unable to move more than that.

"No, not a witch. I'm a dark fae in my realm. Queen Mab to the fae, the Winter Court, to be precise. If I were mortal, perhaps I would have returned with you to your cottage, but alas, I'm hungry and am due back to the Faerie Realm."

Gretel… Gretel… His sister had been here, and this monster had *devoured* her.

Hansel had been too lost in pleasure, knowing he should have fought harder to leave. The fact that Gretel had died before he set out on his mission was no comfort at all. He shoved his emotions down, tucked the memories of Gretel away for now—he'd failed her in the end. Hansel finally found the strength to move, but Mab's hand was at his neck, fingers like steel crushing his throat as she slammed him against the wall. Flames burned up and across his flesh as though he was lit on fire, but there wasn't an orange flame in sight. There was no escape, nothing he could do while his body writhed in pain, his insides melting.

Mab then licked her lips, her nostrils flaring, and her dark eyes sparkling with anticipation as she prepared for her feast.

Him.

Asher

Thorna,

Thank you for your lovely and deliciously dark tales. I wrote these two pieces for you and the butterflies watched me as I did so. They seemed to think the shorts weren't completely awful, so hopefully you agree. And if not, it's my turn to kiss, touch, and taste every inch of you tonight.

#1

I thump. I beat. I pump. A chest consumes my entire being. I'm surrounded by a sternum and two lungs, holding me prisoner. Her sound calls to me, but she's hidden, too. Blood slithers and slides inside me, around me. Her pounding grows louder, and I need the precious song she sings. These layers and layers of membranes and muscles hold me back—a suit of skin I cannot slice through. For a moment, the suit of armor I'm buried in drifts closer to her person's coating. She presses forward to touch me…

But then she's gone.

#2

Colors flow through us, around us, inside us. Some days I choose to be purple, while other days I want to be green or yellow or red—maybe a combination thereof. As colors we can interweave and glide into shapes—falling together, holding ourselves together. We mingle, we love, we gather, we fold into one—as one. The dark lights up with any of us, while the obsidian protects and hides us. We are not only one, but many laced inside a web that will not be shredded, broken, or frayed.

Because the world is ours.

Love you through immortality,
Asher

Thank you so much for reading These Vicious Thorns! Authors always appreciate reviews, whether long or short.

Subscribe to Candace's Awesome Newsletter for the latest news and giveaways!

Check out Candace's other books!

Wicked Souls Duology
Vault of Glass
Bride of Glass

Marked by Magic
The Bone Valley
Merciless Stars

Cruel Curses Trilogy
Clouded By Envy
Veiled By Desire
Shadowed By Despair

Faeries of Oz Series
Lion (Short Story Prequel)
Tin
Crow
Ozma
Tik-Tok

Cursed Hearts Duology
Lyrics & Curses

Music & Mirrors

Immortal Letters Duology
Dearest Clementine: Dark and Romantic Monstrous
Tales
Dearest Dorin: A Romantic Ghostly Tale

Campfire Fantasy Tales Series
Lullaby of Flames
A Layer Hidden
The Celebration Game
Mirror, Mirror

These Vicious Thorns: Tales of the Lovely Grim
Between the Quiet
Hearts Are Like Balloons
Bacon Pie
Avocado Bliss

Vampires in Wonderland Series
Rav (Short Story Prequel)
Maddie
Chess
Knave

Demons of Frosteria
Frost Mate (Prequel Novella)
Frost Claim

Acknowledgments

I wanted to thank everyone who chose to pick up this anthology. Some of these stories may seem to not have the happiest of endings, but I promise you they do. Even if the words are finished, the characters' stories are not. So I leave what happens next to you. A butterfly is said to not start out as a beautiful creature, but I believe a caterpillar is equally beautiful. A big shout out to Amber H., Elle, Donna, Amber D., Jerica, and Vic for helping me with these stories over the years. Now I want you to think about where your story is now and where you want it to lead you, dear friend.

About the Author

Candace Robinson spends her days consumed by words and hoping to one day find her own DeLorean time machine. Her life consists of avoiding migraines, admiring Bonsai trees, watching classic movies, and living with her husband and daughter in Texas—where it can be forty degrees one day and eighty the next.